Something in the Way He Needs

"For anyone with a kinkier bone in their body, this is going to be a great read!"

—Spectrum Books

"This story really had a lot of great ups and interesting downs for the characters but I quite enjoyed the emotional rollercoaster."

—Lily Mac's Blog

"This is a story not to be missed if you love… a great story, brilliant characters and a very happy ending, I highly recommend this book to everyone."

—MM Good Book Reviews

Strong Enough

"*Strong Enough* is lovely, sexy and sweet; it is an easy to read… most of us will happily succumb to the author's compelling story of true love."

—Queer Town Abbey

"I thoroughly enjoyed this sexy and romantic story where love flowed easily between two good men while they found their place in each other's lives. Another fantastic treat from Cardeno C., who has quickly become one of my favorite authors."

—The Romance Reviews

More Than Everything

"Cardeno C. can weave a wonderful story full of emotion and hot, hot sex, and she doesn't disappoint in *More Than Everything*."

—Prism Book Alliance

"Truly a hidden gem that pulled me out of a book funk!"

—Shh Moms Reading

By CARDENO C.

All of Me
Control *with Mary Calmes*
Eight Days
Grand Adventures (Dreamspinner Anthology)
In Another Life
Perfect Imperfections
Places in Time
A Shot at Forgiveness

THE FAMILY SERIES
Something in the Way He Needs
Strong Enough
More Than Everything
The Half of Us

THE HOME SERIES
Home Again
He Completes Me
Where He Ends and I Begin
Love at First Sight
Just What the Truth Is
The One Who Saves Me
Marriage: A Home Series Celebration
Home Again/A Shot at Forgiveness (Anthology)
Walk With Me

THE MATES SERIES
Wake Me Up Inside
Until Forever Comes
In Your Eyes

Published by DREAMSPINNER PRESS
http://www.dreamspinnerpress.com

THE HALF OF US

CARDENO C.

A BOOK IN THE Family SERIES

Dreamspinner Press

Published by
DREAMSPINNER PRESS

5032 Capital Circle SW, Suite 2, PMB# 279, Tallahassee, FL 32305-7886 USA
http://www.dreamspinnerpress.com/

This is a work of fiction. Names, characters, places, and incidents either are the product of author imagination or are used fictitiously, and any resemblance to actual persons, living or dead, business establishments, events, or locales is entirely coincidental.

The Half of Us
© 2014 Cardeno C.

Cover Art
© 2014 Reese Dante.
www.reesedante.com
Cover content is for illustrative purposes only and any person depicted on the cover is a model.

ISBN: 978-1-63216-385-1
Digital ISBN: 978-1-63216-386-8
Library of Congress Control Number: 2014947601
First Edition October 2014

Printed in the United States of America
♾
This paper meets the requirements of
ANSI/NISO Z39.48-1992 (Permanence of Paper).

To Cherie Noel and Portia de Moncur: Thank you so very much for reading this book and lending me your expertise. I'm very grateful.

To Kris: Thanks for all that you do.

To Angela Stiver: Thank you for your kindness and your lovely decorations.

To Kelly Shorten: You're the best web designer around, and I can never say thanks enough.

To Jason Mitchell: Thank you for your friendship and for being a voracious reader.

To Reese Dante: Thanks once again for an amazing cover.

THE HALF OF US

Chapter 1

"THERE'S NOTHING anyone could have done."

Jason Garcia dipped his chin in acknowledgment of the comment, but didn't slow his pace or look at the anesthesiologist walking alongside him.

"The patient's thoracic aorta was dissected. His coronary artery was lacerated. And he had several pulmonary contusions. Nobody could have survived that. The only mystery is how he stayed alive long enough to make it onto the table."

Hearing Dr. Mason recite injuries the patient sustained when his Prius collided with a Range Rover going eighty miles an hour on roads slick with early September rain was nothing short of annoying. Jason wanted to point out that as the cardiothoracic surgeon on the case, he had in fact been in the operating room, so he didn't need the instructional on the injuries. But he didn't want to say or do anything to extend the conversation, so instead he grunted.

"I know how rough it is to lose one." Dr. Mason put his hand on Jason's shoulder in what was probably supposed to be a comforting gesture but wasn't. "I'm off right now too. Do you want to get a drink and talk about it?"

Surprised by the question, Jason turned his head to look at Dr. Mason. What on earth did he think they could talk about? The patient was dead. Jason hadn't been able to save him. No amount of conversation was going to change that.

"I have plans." Jason took the final step toward the physicians' locker room, grasped the doorknob, and said, "Thanks for the offer," as he stepped inside.

"Oh." Dr. Mason followed him. "At this hour?"

Jason flicked his gaze to the clock above the lockers and saw it was after midnight. Late, but still plenty of time to shower, change, drive to a nearby bar, and pick up somebody he could use to fuck away the memory of the day. He had been doing that more often than not lately. When he thought about how differently his life had turned out from what he'd worked and hoped for, he inevitably ended up in more bars looking for more liquor and more sex in the hope of forgetting that realization. It was a vicious cycle, but at least he was getting laid.

"Yes, at this hour," he said without elaborating further. He opened his locker, quickly shrugged off his clothes, and then stuffed them into the front pocket of his bag. "Have a good night." He hurried to the shower, waving to Dr. Mason over his shoulder.

After making quick work of scrubbing down his body and washing his hair, Jason snagged one of the towels from the shelf and dried off. At thirty-six, he was still in decent shape, his arms defined and his chest and belly tight enough to look good under clothes. Silver now streaked his black hair at the temples, and small lines had formed next to his brown eyes, but the places he went were dark enough that nobody noticed. Though he couldn't pass for being in his twenties and he didn't get swarmed at the bars, Jason generally had no trouble finding what he wanted—a warm body to distract him for an hour, maybe two, when the only thing waiting for him was an empty house and the promise of another workday.

He got into his car, drove onto the 15, and headed toward his favorite places to troll—the bars close to the Strip. Guys in town for conferences invariably followed the "what happens in Vegas, stays in Vegas" motto and went out with the purpose of getting laid. Names, if they gave them, were first names only and more likely than not fake. Phone numbers weren't discussed. And hotel rooms were conveniently located for a quick in and a seamless out.

At ten minutes, the drive from the hospital to the bar wasn't long enough for Jason to clear his mind, let alone get rid of the rock-sized ache in the pit of his stomach that came every time he lost a patient, but he figured a couple of drinks and a blow job would do the trick. He climbed out of his black Mercedes E-Class convertible, straightened his oxford and starched jeans, and walked inside.

Dim lights, musky smell, men crowded around a bar chatting or calling for drinks, and two tables in the corner occupied by women celebrating a bachelorette party—a typical Friday night at the Phoenix. Jason hadn't yet reached the bar to order his usual rum and Coke when a laugh distracted him. It wasn't particularly loud, but the joy in it cut through the noise in the room and caught his attention.

Slowly, Jason turned in a circle as he narrowed his eyes and looked around, trying to find the source of the warm sound. He had almost made it back to his starting position when he heard it again, coming from the seating area tucked between the bar and the tiny stage. A group of men were squished together on the leather sofa, the table in front of them lined with empty glasses. One of them kept trying to get up, only to have his friends tug him back down.

Before he thought about what he was doing, Jason walked toward them.

"You guys, seriously, I have to go," the guy said, still sounding amused.

"It's early!" one of his friends yelled. At the same time, another said, "You never go out with us!" And a third shouted, "But it's your birthday!"

"It's almost one in the morning. I went out with you tonight. And it's no longer my birthday." He stood up again, wriggled out of his friends' grasps, and started climbing over their legs.

"What, no good-bye kiss?" one man said. Another made exaggerated smooching noises.

The guy rolled his eyes and smiled. "Thanks for tonight. It was fun."

"Come on, Abe, stay!"

He shook his head as he carefully made his way out of the tangled mess of bodies. "I have to be up early tomorrow."

Jason had heard enough to know he should find someone else to screw. This guy—Abe—was done for the night. But before Jason could move away, Abe finally extricated himself from his friends and Jason got a closer look at him.

His hair was blond, straight, a little too long, and silky. Light-colored eyes framed by thin eyebrows dominated his face. He was a few inches shorter than Jason's six foot one, which put him at about five foot eight. And he was young. Not so young that he wasn't legal, but Jason was sure he had at least a decade on the good-looking man.

All indications—Abe's age, his appearance, and his comments to his friends—indicated a straight path toward rejection and therefore a waste of Jason's time. And yet, when Abe stumbled as he left the seating area, Jason lunged forward and grabbed him.

"Careful," he said. "It's crowded in here tonight."

"Thanks." Abe clutched his shirt and blinked up at him.

Blue. His eyes were blue.

"Anytime." It was the kind of thing he'd say automatically, without thinking and without meaning it. But he did mean it. In fact, it was possibly the most sincere statement he'd made that day.

After a few breaths, Abe released Jason's shirt and stepped away. "Thanks again," he said, rubbing his chest.

Jason turned around and watched the small, round ass in the tight jeans get swallowed by the crowd. Dammit, the guy was hot. Seriously hot. And, sure, he wasn't Jason's normal type, but that was only because Jason's normal type was drunk, desperate, and horny.

Nothing ventured, nothing gained, he told himself as he followed the seemingly sober, likely never desperate, and apparently not horny guy heading toward the exit.

By the time Jason reached Abe, he was dialing his phone in a semiempty nook next to the door.

"Meeting someone?" Jason asked.

Abe flipped around and jerked his gaze to Jason's.

"Sorry. I didn't mean to scare you."

"Not scared. Startled." Abe smiled, the expression as warm as his laugh. "And no." He held up his phone. "It's too late to meet anyone. I'm calling a cab."

"I'll give you a ride."

"You will?" Abe arched his eyebrows. "Do we know each other?"

Jason shook his head.

"So why do you…." Abe ducked his chin and then glanced up, his upper teeth pressing into his lower lip. "Oh."

Shyness wasn't a turn-on for Jason because he rarely had the time or the inclination to seduce or cajole or whatever label people put on trying to get into someone's pants. When he was out looking, he wanted a guy who was in it for the same thing. Sex. In, out, done. Simple, satisfying, and over. But he had to admit to himself that on Abe, shy became sweet and attractive.

"I'm Jason." He held his hand out.

After looking down, Abe put his palm in Jason's. "I'm Abraham. Abe."

"Nice to meet you, Abe."

They shook hands, but rather than let go right away, Abe linked their fingers together. Though he wasn't the hand-holding type, Jason didn't pull back. It wasn't as if they were in a place someone would recognize him, which was one of the draws to the bar. Besides, he wanted Abe to accept his offer. They hadn't gotten naked yet, and the tight little body in front of him already had him hard. It promised to be a good night.

"What do you say?" He pulled his keys out of his pocket with his free hand and held them up. "You game?"

Abe looked at him, really looked at him, but not at his body or his groin, which were the usual points of interest. Instead, Abe looked at his face, his lips, and mostly his eyes.

"I never do this," he mumbled, presumably to himself, "but you only live once, right?" He took in a deep breath. "How much have you had to drink?"

Taken aback by the question, Jason said, "Nothing yet. I just got here. Why?"

"Because going home with some guy I've never met is about as risky as I'm willing to get for one night. If you're drunk, we're both getting in a cab."

"I'm not drunk."

"I can't believe I'm doing this," Abe said under his breath. Then he nodded and squared his shoulders. "Okay."

A yes was a yes. Wanting to get out of there before Abe changed his mind, Jason rested his palm on Abe's lower back and steered him out of the bar. "I'm parked right over there." He pointed his key fob toward his Mercedes and unlocked the door.

Most guys had some reaction to his car. If not an outright compliment, then at least the appearance of being impressed. It was why he'd bought a car that cost more than some houses. Abe didn't seem to notice.

"Your place or mine?" Abe said once they got into the car. He grinned and waggled his eyebrows, his expression playful. "I never thought I'd get the chance to say that."

Jason found himself laughing, which was rare in general and never happened with tricks. Maybe it was because he was completely sober.

"Yours. I live pretty far." The familiar lie came easily. "Where are you staying?"

"Staying?" Abe buckled up his seat belt.

"Uh-huh." Jason backed out of the parking space. "Which hotel?"

"Oh." Abe shook his head. "I live here. Well, not here, but in Henderson. Is that too far?"

At that time of night, it was less than half an hour. A fact Jason knew because he lived in Henderson too.

"No. It's fine." He pulled out of the parking lot.

"So," Abe said.

Jason jerked his gaze over to Abe and then back to the road.

"I don't usually do this sort of thing. Want to tell me how it goes?"

Furrowing his brow, Jason tried to think of how to respond and came up empty.

"No? All right." Abe cleared his throat. "Small talk, then. Did you grow up in Vegas or are you a transplant?"

Small talk. That was new. Then again, they had some time to kill.

"I grew up in Reno," Jason said. "How about you?"

"I'm from Utah originally. Salt Lake. But I moved here for school."

And with that, Abe was off, chatting about where he went to college (UNLV), his parents (divorced), his sister (four kids, lived in Idaho), why he moved to Las Vegas (good weather, less conservative than his hometown), and other equally mundane topics. Jason was able to ward off most personal questions with a grunt, so the conversation wasn't painful. Actually, if he was honest with himself, it was nice. Listening to Abe chatter allowed him to focus on something other than work or the state of his own life, which was relaxing. Before he knew it, they were getting off the freeway and Abe was giving him directions to his apartment interspersed with tidbits about the area.

"Pass the grocery store. Doesn't it look great? They just remodeled the whole strip mall and the inside of the store. They added a nut bar with all sorts of different nuts that you can grind to make fresh nut butter. The honey-roasted peanuts are my favorite. I go through a jar every couple of weeks."

Jason glanced at Abe, dragging his gaze up and down his slim body. "Really?" He looked at the road again.

Abe shrugged. "Fast metabolism. Plus, I swim."

"Well, it's working for you," he said, looking at Abe appreciatively. It was getting harder and harder to focus on driving.

Though it was too dark to know if Abe blushed at the compliment, Jason noticed him ducking his chin and biting his lip.

"Make a left at the light after the Roasted Bean. Oh my God, they have the best chai lattes there. I know it seems like they should be the same at every coffee shop, but theirs is special. Plus, refills are half price and they have a bunch of comfy couches and chairs. I've spent many weekend afternoons and evenings camped out there with my laptop or a book."

Jason got an image of Abe curled up on a big sofa, his hair flopping over his forehead, a steaming mug in front of him and a book in his hand. "That sounds nice."

"It is." Abe pointed to an apartment complex just ahead of them. "That's me. Building C."

Jason drove in, parked in front of the building, and turned off the ignition. For the first time in as long as he could remember, he was a little anxious about going to bed with someone. Though he hadn't shared anything about himself and he didn't know all that much about Abe, he no longer felt like a stranger. The last time he'd had sex with someone he knew in any sense of the word, he had been married and trying to convince both himself and his wife that he wanted to stay that way.

"This is kind of weird, isn't it?" Abe asked as they sat in the quiet car.

"No," Jason assured Abe and himself. It was sex. That was a basic bodily need. In, out, done. That was his motto and he followed it religiously. There was nothing weird about it that couldn't be attributed to his current state of sobriety. He made a mental note to never again pick up a guy until after he'd had a couple of drinks. With that decision made, Jason grabbed the door handle. "Ready?"

Abe looked at him again, one of his quiet stares. Jason tried not to wriggle under that scrutiny.

"You're really attractive," Abe said.

Not sure how he was supposed to respond, Jason went with the simple approach. "Thanks." When Abe didn't say anything or make a move to leave the car or stop staring at him, Jason added, "That's a good thing, right?"

"Yes." Abe nodded. "But it's not why I agreed to bring you home." Before Jason could decide if he should probe for an answer, Abe grinned at him and said, "But it sure helped. Come on." He opened his door and stepped out of the car.

It wasn't too late to leave. Jason could put the car in reverse, drive away, and either hit another bar or find someone online who wanted to fuck without talking or laughing or smiling. He had three apps on his phone for just that purpose. But he didn't back away or reach for his phone. Instead, he got out of the car, locked it, and followed Abe into his apartment.

"Nice place," Jason said as soon as he walked inside.

"I haven't turned the lights on yet," Abe answered with a laugh. "You can't see anything. The walls could be fuchsia and mint-green polka dots for all you know."

Jason didn't care about the walls. He cared about getting Abe naked. The comment was something he said just to have something to say. But when Abe turned around and gave him a half hug to take the sting out of his teasing response, Jason found himself grinning and hugging Abe in return.

"What if I like fuchsia and mint green?" he asked. "Those could be my favorite colors."

Crinkling his nose, Abe shifted until he was right in front of Jason, their chests touching. "Hmm. Those are your favorite colors?" He wrapped his arms around Jason's neck, stretched up, and kissed the base of Jason's throat. "I never would have guessed. You seem more like the tan-walls, blue-shirts type."

His walls were in fact tan and the majority of his shirts were in fact blue. Slowly, Jason curled his arms around Abe's waist, and then he goosed him hard.

"Ah!" Abe shouted and tried to move away.

Holding on tight, Jason said, "Not so smug now, are you?"

"I didn't know it was such a sensitive topic." Abe's breath came out faster as he kept trying to escape.

Jason squeezed his ass again for fun and then again because he liked doing it.

"I'll never tell," Abe said. "I promise. Your secret is safe with me."

"Are you making fun of me?" Jason asked, enjoying the interaction more than he would have expected. "Because that seems like an incredibly bad idea." He dug his fingers into Abe's sides. "Tell you what. Just to show you I'm a good guy, I'll let go and give you a sixty-second head start to get to your bedroom. If you manage to get naked in that time, I'll let you off the hook."

"What a gentleman," Abe said breathlessly.

"I'm pretty sure you won't say that after you see what I plan to do to you once I catch you." Jason winked and stepped away. "Time starts now. Go!"

Laughing, Abe swung around. Jason managed to get a good smack onto his ass before he hustled away.

"That's cheating!" Abe said as he ran out of the room.

"Nah." Jason unbuttoned his shirt and sauntered after him. "Cheating is giving you less than sixty seconds." He knocked on

Abe's open bedroom door and walked in to see Abe lying faceup on his bed, still fully clothed, kicking off his shoes.

"That wasn't sixty seconds," Abe said between gasps. Though he was smiling broadly, his voice sounded strained and his chest heaved.

"Are you okay?" Jason asked as he approached the bed. He toed off his own shoes and then climbed up next to Abe and rested his palm on Abe's narrow chest, feeling his heartbeat.

"I'm fine. My asthma acts up in this weather, and it was a long day and"—he lowered his gaze and blushed—"you got me kind of worked up when you were touching me." He licked his lips. "I'm really nervous."

Damn. Abe was sweet. Young and sweet. Jason suddenly felt guilty for being there. Mindless sex with guys who knew the score was what he wanted, not emotional entanglements for himself or the men he fucked.

"Don't leave," Abe said. Apparently, he was good at reading body language or facial expressions. "I want this." He covered Jason's hand with his smaller one. "I want you. Let me just get my inhaler. I have one in the nightstand."

Jason moved back while Abe got his inhaler and took a quick puff. "Better?" he asked.

"Yes." Abe nodded.

Taking a few moments to look at Abe's chest, Jason watched it rise and fall and waited for his breathing to ease. When Abe's breaths were even, Jason laid his hand over Abe's heart again and noticed the bulge in his jeans growing, which made his own groin tighten. Abe said he was fine. A yes was a yes, and Jason was way too turned on to leave. He flicked open the buttons on his wrists and shrugged out of his shirt.

"Get naked," he commanded.

Nodding, Abe crunched up, reached over his shoulders, grasped his shirt, and tugged it over his head. He lay back down, unbuttoned his jeans, arched up, and then shoved them and his briefs off his trim hips and down his legs.

"You have a great body," Jason said, enjoying the view of smooth, pale skin and lithe muscles. Abe's cock was different from his, lighter in color, not as thick or long, and without prominent veins. Jason cupped it, enjoying the weight and heat in his hand. "And a really pretty dick."

Abe lay still, letting Jason touch and explore. A light smattering of fuzz covered his round, tightly drawn balls. Lowering his face, Jason lapped at them, enjoying the texture of the wrinkled skin.

"Oh God," Abe gasped. "You need to slow down. That's too good."

Smirking about the fact he had Abe close to bursting already, Jason dragged his hands down Abe's legs and pushed off his socks. "You're telling me you can't get it up again at your age?" He climbed off the bed, pulled off his own socks, and then dropped his jeans and underwear to the ground. "Speaking of which, how old are you?"

When Abe didn't answer, Jason glanced up to find red lips parted and blue eyes staring at his cock. It'd take someone without much ego to remain nonchalant in the face of that admiring expression, and nobody had ever accused Jason of lacking when it came to the ego department. Or the dick department, which seemed to be making Abe very happy.

"Abe?"

Without raising his gaze, Abe licked his lips. "Yeah?"

Chuckling, Jason climbed back onto the bed and knee walked until his groin was inches from Abe's face. "Are you going to answer my question?"

"Question?" Abe finally blinked up at him. "Oh, uh, I'm twenty-six." Slowly, he reached his hand out and wrapped it around Jason's rigid cock. "Damn." He nodded. "And, yeah, I'll get it up again."

That reverent, gentle touch distracted Jason from everything except getting off. "You want to suck me?" He gripped the base of his dick, planted one hand on the bed, and lowered himself over Abe's mouth, painting his lips with his cockhead. "Come on."

Groaning, Abe parted his lips and Jason slid inside. He moved slowly, aware his girth wasn't easy to take, but Abe didn't hesitate. He let Jason set the pace, moaning with arousal as his mouth was filled and even managing to get his tongue involved, flicking it over Jason's heated skin.

"Christ, that's good," Jason rasped.

He removed his hand from his cock and pushed it farther into wet heat, not stopping until Abe gagged. Surprisingly, Abe didn't shove him away. He clutched Jason's hips and held on as Jason moved out and then plunged back in, over and over again. After a couple of minutes, Abe whimpered, the sound aroused rather than pained.

"It's sexy how much this is turning you on," Jason said through gritted teeth. "I'm close."

Abe bucked and moaned, drawing Jason's attention to his swollen cock. He flipped around and in one move, thrust deeper into Abe's mouth and sucked Abe's dick between his lips. The thin body underneath him went wild, shaking and moaning, gripping him hard enough to bruise and sucking with desperation.

"Ungh," Jason moaned when early seed seeped onto his tongue. He played too much to swallow, so he pulled back regretfully. "That's it," he said as he stroked Abe, still rocking in and out of his mouth. "Give it to me."

Within seconds, Abe arched and cried out around Jason's cock as he shot into Jason's fist. The scent, the sounds, and the sight of that pretty dick releasing a load, tipped Jason over the edge. He barely had time to pull out and start jacking himself before he was grunting his way through his own orgasm, painting Abe's chin, neck, and chest with his seed. The pleasure seemed to last forever, his breath gone and his balls aching by the time he was spent.

"Jesus," he said as he collapsed, his leg thrown across Abe's chest and his face resting on Abe's flat belly.

"Good," Abe said as he patted Jason's head, the motion tired.

Not knowing if it was a question or a statement, Jason said, "Uh-huh," and then he kissed Abe's hip. Really good. Damn.

"I need to get some water before we go again," Jason mumbled after a few minutes. He sat up with a sigh and turned to Abe. "Do you want…?"

Abe's eyes were closed, his lips were tilted up in a satisfied smile, his hair was mussed, and his cheeks were flushed. He was breathing evenly, deeply, already fast asleep. No way could Jason wake him when he looked so cozy.

After nuzzling his face in Abe's groin, inhaling his arousing scent, and committing it to memory, Jason got out of bed and gathered his clothes. He didn't do the same guy twice, not ever, but the sweet blond almost had him leaving his number. *Almost*.

Chapter 2

ABE FOLLOWED his friend Thad into the Phoenix. After a week's
worth of late nights preparing report cards, the quarter finally ended
and he was ready to unwind.

"Thad, Abe, over here!" their friends called out and waved.

Stress melted away and Abe smiled, happy to be out with
adults. "Hey," he said as he reached the table. He looked at the
empty glasses covering almost every square inch and arched his
eyebrows. "How long have you been here? I thought we were
meeting at nine. We're not that late, are we?"

"Nah. We just got here. It's busy, so we grabbed the table
when the guys who were here before us left. Nobody's bussed it
yet."

Abe looked around the bar. Only nine o'clock and it was
already packed. Apparently the Phoenix was the place to go on
Saturdays. He didn't go out enough to know which bars were
popular on which nights. Not that it mattered. He planned to sit with
his friends, have a couple of drinks, and catch up. Hanging out at
someone's house would have been just as fun, but Thad liked going
out and being seen. Well, as long as he was there, he'd make the
most of it.

"Who wants a drink?" he said. "I'm going to the bar." His
friends called out their orders, and he smiled and turned around.

"That's a lot of drinks. I'll go with you." Thad stood up next to Abe and leaned close as they walked away from the table. "There's a guy at the bar who looks good enough to eat."

"If you're eating Bar Guy, how are you planning to help me carry the drinks?" Abe asked with a smile.

"If Bar Guy lets me eat him, you're on your own with the drinks."

"You'd abandon me with an armful of drinks after I came here for you?" Abe said in mock horror. "That's heartless."

"The guy's *really* hot and—" Thad stopped midsentence, dipped his chin, and quietly hissed, "That's him. He's looking at me, right? I mean, don't look, but he's looking at me, right?"

A cute guy at the bar was glancing in their direction, so Abe said, "Yes."

"Okay." Thad straightened his shoulders. "I'm going for it. Wish me luck."

"Good luck," Abe said with a laugh.

"Did you see that?" Thad asked as he stumbled.

"What?"

"He just winked at me and grabbed his dick." He smiled broadly and sauntered away. "Forget luck. This one's in the bag. I'll call you tomorrow."

Having grown up in Utah, Abe had been surprised by the openness and promiscuity he'd witnessed when he moved to Las Vegas. But after living there for seven years, making friends with people from all over, and having a couple of short-term relationships, very little fazed him.

Plus, he now had a firsthand understanding of the appeal of going home with a hot guy. He had made it his birthday present to himself a couple of months earlier, when he'd taken home a man with sad eyes, a handsome face, and a talented body. And even though Abe had been disappointed when he'd woken up alone the next morning, he had no regrets. It wasn't something he'd make a habit of—he was built for relationships, not hookups—but he'd had fun that night and the sex had been…. The memory made his heart speed up and his dick swell.

"Hi. Abe, right?" a deep voice said from behind him.

The voice sounded like Jason's, and Abe's first thought was that he must be hearing things. When he felt a big hand on his shoulder, he knew someone was behind him, but he figured thinking of the man had him attributing his voice to someone else. Then he swung around.

"Jason," Abe moaned. He swallowed thickly and tried to slow his suddenly rapid breathing. "Hi."

"I thought that was you." Jason slowly moved his palm down Abe's arm. "You remember me too, huh?"

"I, uh, have a decent memory and you made a pretty good impression."

"Pretty good?"

Feeling his cheeks heat, Abe ducked his head and ignored the question. "How've you been?"

"Fine." Jason kept slowly moving his palm until he reached Abe's hand, and then he curled his fingers around Abe's. "Better now. Let's get out of here."

The feeling of Jason's hot skin, the sound of his husky voice, and the sight of his broad body had Abe's senses reeling. He remembered how good it felt to be touched by this man. He had never cum so hard or had it last so long. Of course, he had never been tossed aside so quickly, either. He harbored no ill will toward Jason because he'd known going in how the night would end, but that didn't mean he wanted a repeat of waking up alone the morning after.

"I don't do that," Abe said.

"As I recall, you do it really, really well."

Though he was glad the pleasure from that night hadn't been one-sided, the compliment wouldn't hold him all night or kiss him good morning. "That was a one-time thing," Abe explained. "Look, I had fun, but I don't do hookups."

He raised his gaze, wanting to give Jason the respect of looking him in the eyes when he turned him down. Right away, he realized that had been a mistake. But once he connected with that dark gaze, he couldn't turn away. Jason's eyes were why he had agreed to take him home the last time. Deep, intelligent, lonely eyes.

"I only do one-time things, so I get that," Jason admitted without letting go of Abe's hand and without walking away. He moved his thumb back and forth over Abe's wrist. "I shouldn't have come over here, shouldn't have asked you to go to bed with me again, but…."

Abe looked at him and waited for him to finish the sentence. "But?" he repeated.

The sides of Jason's mouth turned up, and he shrugged. "But I want you."

That feeling was most definitely mutual, and it had Abe questioning whether he should follow his gut, ignore his brain, and take Jason home again. They'd already had sex once, what difference would another time make? It was an excuse, a rationalization, and he knew it. Torn, he bit his lip and looked at Jason, hoping for… something.

"You promised me another round and then you fell asleep," Jason reminded him. "So actually, this would be a continuation of the other night."

"Are you saying we only had half last time, so there's another half before we exhaust the one time?"

"If that's what I meant, would it convince you to say yes?"

Abe taught math for a living, so he had to smile at that particular type of cajoling. "I think it might." He turned his palm and clutched Jason's hand.

"Oh, good. I'm glad I went with that instead of my other convincing idea."

"What was the other one going to be?" Abe asked.

Jason cleared his throat and in an exaggeratedly seductive voice said, "Hey, sugar. I have a box of condoms that's about to expire and I'd hate to throw it in a landfill. Do you want to come save the planet with me?"

Abe barked out a laugh. "That definitely wouldn't have worked."

"No?" Jason smiled at him. "Then I'm glad I went with the first one."

Abe was glad too. "You drove again?"

"Yes. And like last time, I just got here, so I'm sober."

Hearing that Jason remembered what he'd said two months prior made Abe feel less like a disposable hookup and more like a human being who mattered at some level. His tension eased.

"Give me a minute to tell my friends I'm leaving, and then I'll meet you out front." Abe started to walk away but stopped when Jason didn't release his hand. He glanced down at their joined fingers and then up at Jason.

"It's pretty crowded in here. Maybe you should text them instead."

After a few seconds of frowning as he wondered what Jason was up to, Abe's chest clenched in sympathy. "You're worried I'm making an excuse and I won't come back."

"No, I'm not," Jason said, but the fact that he averted his gaze and the gulping motion of his Adam's apple belied that statement. "Like I said, it's crowded in here."

"Okay," Abe agreed as he fished his phone out of his pocket. "I'll text them." Jason let go of his hand, and Abe looked down at his phone, shielding his pleased smile from Jason's view. He didn't want to make the gruff guy think he was laughing at him. "All done," he said once he'd sent the message and neutralized his expression. "My place again?"

Jason nodded, put his hand on Abe's lower back, and steered them toward the door.

THE CAR ride to his apartment was strangely normal. Like last time, Abe spent most of the time rambling nervously. Jason was quiet, and it hadn't escaped Abe's attention that he didn't share many details about himself, like, for example, his last name. But Abe learned bits and pieces of information—Jason was a doctor, he liked classical rock music, he loved red meat but tried to eat chicken and fish instead for health reasons, he enjoyed cooking but didn't do much of it. None of the details were earth-shattering, but together they sketched a picture of the strong, stoic man whose eyes showed hidden vulnerability.

Knowing something about the person he was going to have sex with made Abe a little less nervous. The memory of how good it had been helped too. So this time around, when Jason pulled into his parking lot, Abe didn't hesitate to get out of the car. They walked to the apartment side by side, brushing against each other more often than not.

Once they were inside with the door closed and locked behind them, Abe looked up at Jason. The light from one table lamp provided the only illumination in the room and left portions of Jason's face in shadows. Abe ran his fingers over Jason's prominent jawline and stepped closer.

"If you want to hang out and talk, or if you want something to eat or drink, let me know."

Jason shook his head, pressed his palm to Abe's chest, and rubbed his thumb over his nipple, making him gasp and then moan.

"Do you remember where my bedroom is?" Abe asked breathlessly.

"I remember everything from that night." Jason stopped moving his thumb, stopped speaking, possibly even stopped breathing after that confession.

Not sure if ignoring the comment was better than acknowledging it, Abe went with telling the truth. "I do too." He stepped closer to Jason and wrapped his arms around his waist.

After a moment of hesitation, Jason returned the gesture, curling his arm around Abe's back and tugging him into a hug. They stood together, neither speaking, and Abe relaxed into Jason's embrace. Rather than pulling away or moving them into the bedroom, Jason held him close and eventually began combing his fingers through Abe's hair.

"This is nice," Abe whispered, not wanting to disrupt the peacefulness of the moment, the intimacy.

"Uh-huh."

"Do you dance?"

"I haven't in a while, but I'm not bad at it. Why?"

Abe shrugged and cuddled in closer. "This is a little like dancing, you know?"

Dragging one hand down Abe's back and caressing his nape with the other, Jason said, "It sure is."

Abe wanted to ask Jason to go out with him again, to go dancing. But then he remembered it wouldn't be *again* because they weren't on a date. It wasn't exactly what he wanted, but Abe was enjoying himself. As he rested his head on Jason's chest, he was serenaded by the steady beat of his heart, enveloped by heat and strength, and surrounded by the scent of Jason's skin and soap. By the time Jason suggested moving to the bedroom, Abe was ready. Comfortable, warm, and aroused, he looked forward to another night in bed with a sexy man, despite the fact that he'd made no secret of his plan to be gone in the morning.

"I'm glad I ran into you tonight," Abe said as he leaned against his bedroom wall and tugged Jason's shirt out of his pants.

"Mmm, me too." Jason hunched down and licked and nibbled on Abe's neck while he worked his jeans open. "I wasn't sure it was you at first, but then you laughed and I knew." He shoved his hand down the front of Abe's jeans and cupped his package as he pushed the jeans and briefs down, leaving them pooled around Abe's feet.

Trembling, Abe clutched Jason's arms and tried to catch his breath. "I swear to God, you touch me and I turn into a teenager again."

"I like touching you." Jason moved the heel of his hand up Abe's cock and then down to his balls.

"Yeah, I like it too. That's the problem."

"Feeling good isn't a problem." Jason licked a path up Abe's neck, nipped his ear, and slid his free hand around to his ass. "Let yourself enjoy it."

When Jason wiggled his fingers into Abe's crease, Abe threw his head back and swallowed hard. "Don't want it to end too soon."

"I'll get you up again." Jason dragged his teeth over the exposed expanse of Abe's neck. "Goddamn, you feel good."

"Yes. I…. Yes," Abe mumbled incoherently.

Jason steadily stroked Abe's cock while he pressed one finger against his pucker, rubbing in circles.

"Ah!" Abe's eyes widened just as Jason pushed the tip of his finger inside. "Ah!" He went up on tiptoe, taking in Jason's fierce expression and falling into his dark stare.

"Ready?" Jason rasped, his voice hoarse.

Before Abe could figure out what he meant, Jason pushed his finger all the way into Abe's hole and twisted his palm around Abe's cockhead.

"Jase!" Abe cried out, looking into Jason's eyes as he came, spilling over his long, thick fingers.

"That's it." Jason nudged his finger inside, pressing against Abe's gland and drawing out his pleasure. "Give me everything."

With a silent gasp, Abe's cock pulsed again, dribbling out more release. Spent and boneless, he slumped against Jason's chest, his body strumming with pleasure and his mind fuzzy. Still floating, Abe barely noticed Jason picking him up and carrying him to the bed. He raised his arms when Jason nudged them, shivering after his shirt was pulled over his head. It wasn't long before the cold air in the room was replaced by hot skin sliding over him.

"Hey," Jason said as he brushed Abe's hair off his forehead.

Abe blinked and met Jason's gaze. Jason was lying on top of him, smiling softly. Both of them were nude, and the hair on Jason's chest gave Abe added sensation as it brushed against him.

"Are you back to the land of the coherent?"

"That was...." Abe swallowed hard and tried to think of the right word. "Wow."

"Good one, huh?" Jason's smile was self-satisfied, proud, and well-deserved.

Staring at Jason, Abe nodded. He didn't have a lot of experience, but seriously, wow.

"So," Jason said, his expression wicked but his touch gentle as he combed his fingers through Abe's hair. "What do you want to do next?"

Chapter 3

"WHAT'S UP with you?"

Jason looked across the table at his cousin Asher. "What do you mean?"

"You look like someone pissed on your puppy."

"I think the saying is 'pissed on your cereal' or 'kicked your puppy,'" Jason corrected.

The look Asher gave him clearly indicated that the explanation wasn't appreciated. And that he thought Jason was an idiot. It was like being a kid again, except his mother and aunt, Asher's mother, weren't in the next room chatting. Their mothers were close, so they'd spent a lot of time together as children, but Asher lived in San Francisco now, so Jason only got to see him when he was in San Francisco for conferences.

"Nothing's up." Jason reached for his beer. "It's just the holidays. You know how it is."

People got down during that time of year. It was normal. And nothing was better for chasing away the blues than sex, so it made sense that Jason subconsciously went to a place where he'd spent a couple of hot nights. That was what he told himself when he kept missing his turnoff on the freeway and ended up driving by Abe's apartment. It had happened four times that month. So far, he hadn't pulled into the parking lot, let alone gone to the door, but he'd thought about it.

"How what is?" Asher asked.

"The holidays," he repeated. "They're hard on people."

Asher furrowed his brow. "Are you having a big shindig at your place for Christmas or something?"

Jason lived in a sparsely furnished townhouse. A nice townhouse, sure. Three stories, three bedrooms, twenty-five hundred square feet. But it wasn't a place where he'd throw a party even if he were the type to have parties, which he wasn't.

"No." He shook his head.

"Then what's the big stress? Thanksgiving's over. You have a week left to buy Christmas presents." Asher's phone beeped. He picked it up, smiled, and then set it back on the table. "Hell, if you've got time after your conference is over tomorrow, there are a few decent stores around your hotel. Go grab what you need and call it done."

"Was that Daniel?" Jason asked.

"Yeah. He said to tell you he's sorry, but he won't be able to join us for dinner. His brother's latest girlfriend dumped him, so Daniel's at his place, listening to him whine." Asher grimaced. "Have I mentioned how glad I am you're in town so I don't have to be there?"

"I thought you were good friends with his brother. Didn't he introduce the two of you?"

"No, he didn't, and yes, I am. But I have to listen to Ollie's shit at work. If he asks why he can't make a relationship last and then immediately changes the topic one more time, I'm going to break his nose."

There was no way to know if Asher was serious about that threat. It was definitely possible.

"Let me ask you something," Jason said, looking down as he rolled his beer bottle between his palms. "What's it like to be in a relationship?"

Jason had always considered his older cousin the permanently single type, so he had been surprised when he heard Asher had moved a man into his apartment. He had been even more surprised when, a few years later, they were still together.

"You were married for, what, ten years?" Asher asked.

"About that long, yes."

"So I assume you know the answer to your question."

"It was different." Jason started picking at the label on the bottle.

"Yeah, I get that." Asher stretched his long arms across the bench seat. "Angela's great, but if women don't do it for you, that deal was doomed from the start."

It was a succinct explanation of the single biggest failure of Jason's life. "Right," he said.

"So you met a guy?" Asher asked.

Jason jerked his gaze up in surprise. "No."

"No?" Asher arched his eyebrows disbelievingly.

He had slept with one man two times. That didn't constitute anything in the neighborhood of a relationship. Still, Jason would be lying if he said the reason for his question wasn't his desire to make it three times, and maybe more than that. Abe was sexy as hell and sweet as sin, all at the same time. Jason couldn't remember enjoying being with anyone more.

"No." He raised his gaze and met Asher's. "Don't take this the wrong way, but I really don't get the relationship thing."

"You don't *get* the relationship thing?" Asher repeated. "What do you mean, like, for you? Or in general?"

"Not in general, but with two guys." He raised his bottle to his mouth, took a swig, then said, "What's the point?"

"I have no clue what you're talking about."

"Look, I know it's not popular to say it with everyone shouting about equality this and marriage that, but the reality is, you and Daniel aren't going to have kids, you aren't going to limit your sex life to just each other, and you'll be lucky if you're together for five years, let alone fifty. There's no woman pushing for a ring." He shrugged. "Why bother?"

"Damn, man." Asher shook his head. "That is a seriously fucked-up attitude."

"It's an honest observation. And are you saying I'm wrong?" Jason leaned forward. "Just between us. No political posturing, no boyfriend listening, no mother on the phone saying she's worried about you. You're telling me I'm not right about every single one of those things?"

"You're right," Asher said, his expression turning sympathetic. "But only about one thing. We're not having kids. Daniel says taking care of me is a full-time job, and I'm too selfish to want to share him with anyone. But, damn, Jason, the rest of it...." Asher shook his head. "I don't fuck around on him. He doesn't fuck around on me. And, yes, we will be together in five years, and if I live long enough, in fifty, which is why we got married."

Jason's jaw dropped. "You're married?"

Asher nodded.

"Why didn't I know about that?"

"Because we didn't have a fancy wedding. Daniel hates people looking at him, and I didn't give a shit about anything except making him mine every way I could, so we went to city hall."

"You're willing to sacrifice variety and excitement for *that*?"

"It's not a sacrifice. It's a choice. And what's variety?" Asher asked. "Going to bars and hoping to find someone who wants to fuck for a night? I've done that. I'm forty-two years old. I've fucked more guys than I can remember. You think that's variety? Why? We didn't invent fucking. It was around before we were alive and it'll be around after. Doing it with someone new doesn't make it exciting. Exciting is being more than a convenient cock. Exciting is finding new ways to make *my* guy smile. Exciting is getting home and having Daniel look at me like that's the best part of his day."

Hearing his always harsh, never sensitive cousin gush stunned Jason into silence. It also put his brain into overdrive. He had a lot to think about. Not knowing what to say, he nodded.

Asher took in a deep breath, and when he spoke again, his voice was lower, calmer. "Look, everyone has his own boat, and if yours gets floated by something else, that's your thing. But those people you were talking about? The ones shouting about marriage? It means something to them. They want what your parents have. I get that you'd rather lose your left nut than set up house with someone, but don't assume every gay guy thinks like you."

Ironically, Asher was wrong. Jason had lived his entire life wanting what his parents had. They had been married for fifty-five years and still adored each other. He had wanted that type of relationship so much he had told himself it was worth sacrificing anything to get it. Unfortunately, he wasn't great at sacrificing, and his weakness had destroyed his marriage and with it the opportunity to have a close-knit family.

But after listening to his cousin, Jason wondered if maybe he still had a chance for something more than frequent sex with many different people. What he didn't know was what that *something* would look like and what he'd be willing to give up to get it. He picked up his bottle, drained the rest of his beer, and then raised his gaze to meet Asher's.

"I met a guy," he said, contradicting his earlier denial.

"Tell me about him."

He had talked with Abe more than with anyone else he'd gone to bed with, so it made sense that when he heard that question, a fair amount of information came to mind. But what mattered most wasn't any particular fact or anecdote.

"I like being with him," Jason said. "And not just for sex." He paused. "I mean the sex is out of this world, but.... You know what I mean."

Asher nodded but didn't say anything. The silence made it easier for Jason to talk.

"It was supposed to be a one-time thing. Then it turned into two times. And now I keep thinking I want to see him again."

"Sounds easy enough. What's the problem? Did he turn you down?"

"No." Jason picked at the label on his bottle. "But if I keep getting together with him, it'll end up being more than I expected it to be."

"And that's bad?" Asher asked, his tone even, not judgmental.

Was it? Jason didn't know. He shrugged. "Are you going to tell me the only thing to fear is fear itself?"

"I don't write bumper stickers, so no. Besides, I'm a police detective. I've seen a lot of things worth fearing."

Jason smiled lightly. "So are you going to give me advice?"

"Advice?" Asher asked in surprise, as if the word was unfamiliar.

Jason nodded.

"You want advice from me?"

"I don't have anything better to do right now."

"Don't make your e-mail background patterned or colorful. That shit is seriously annoying, and then when you respond, your e-mail is on that pattern." Asher shook his head. "Half the time, I ignore the e-mails based on that alone."

"Very funny," Jason said. "That's not what I meant."

"You want more? Let's see…." Asher picked up his empty beer bottle and rolled it between his palms. "Don't unbutton your shirt all the way down to your rib cage and wear a bunch of gold necklaces in the opening."

Jason snorted. "Anything else?"

"If you pick a guy up, go to his house, and find small pieces of the newspaper cut out, he's probably writing a letter to the press about his latest victim."

"Hmm. So then I have to decide what's more important—the fact that he cares enough about the world around us to be one of the few remaining people with a newspaper subscription, or him being a murderer."

"It's a tough call," Asher said. "Personally, I'd turn around and get the fuck out. Find a guy who likes movies instead."

"I'll take it under advisement," Jason said, shaking his head in amusement. "You have any other golden nuggets to share?"

Asher's expression turned serious. "If you get a chance at happiness, don't squander it."

JASON PLAYED catch-up at work after getting back from his trip to San Francisco, doubling up on his office hours to make up for the time he'd missed and keeping his busy surgery schedule the same. Between that and Christmas, he didn't have much time to do or think about anything else.

But once he was back to his regular schedule, he reflected on what Asher had said about squandering his chance at happiness. The comment hit close to home because it was exactly what Jason knew he had done, not with the cute guy from the bar, but with his marriage.

He wondered if it was really possible to have any version of the life he had wanted but thought he'd lost when his marriage had deteriorated. Or, if he was being honest, well before that.

Marrying another woman was out of the question. Angela was smart, funny, and beautiful, but Jason hadn't been able to make things work with her, so there was no way he'd be able to sustain a relationship with another woman. He'd never considered men an option for anything other than good sex, but after talking with his cousin, he wondered if maybe there was something to the idea of having sex with the same person on a semiregular basis. After all, the second night with Abe had been even better than the first, and they had plenty of positions left to explore.

Hoping if he spent time at the coffee shop Abe frequented, they'd *accidentally* run into each other and he'd have the chance to find out if the third time was in fact the charm, Jason went to the Roasted Bean on Saturday evening. It was the fourth time he'd been there that week, and up to that point, the only thing he'd found out was that the chai latte was as good as Abe had said. The last time he struck out, he'd decided to improve his odds by describing Abe to one of the baristas and asking if she knew when he usually came in. With as frequently as Abe said he went there, Jason had high hopes the barista knew which customer he meant and had armed him with accurate information.

"Was I right? Best chai anywhere, isn't it?"

Jason snapped his gaze up from his phone and met blue eyes. "Abe," he said, not quite as casually as he would have liked. He cleared his throat and got his bearings. "Yes, the latte's great. I might need to get another one." He nudged his chin toward the empty seat across from him. "Join me."

"Uh." Abe flicked his gaze to the chair and then back to Jason. "I don't want to interrupt your evening. I just saw you sitting here, so I came to say hi and see what you thought of the chai." He swallowed hard and turned away. "I'll see you around."

"Wait," Jason said as he jumped to his feet. "You won't be interrupting me."

"Really?" Abe faced him again. His eyebrows were drawn together, and he was chewing his bottom lip. "Are you sure?"

"Definitely." Jason pointed to the chair again. "I'd enjoy the company."

After a moment's hesitation, Abe slowly slid into the chair. He wrapped his palms around his cup and looked down at his drink.

"Are you having the chai too?" Jason asked, trying to make conversation. It was awkward as hell, and he wondered if it was because he was out of practice or if it was because of the situation. People didn't have coffee and make small talk with guys they took home to fuck.

"Yeah. I, uh, have them add a pump of vanilla and a pump of cinnamon to mine." He licked his lips nervously. "It's great."

"That sounds good. I'll try it."

"Sure." Abe pushed his cup halfway across the table.

It took Jason a moment to catch on to the fact that Abe was offering him a taste of the drink. When he said he'd try it, he meant another time, not that he wanted to literally try Abe's drink. Normally, he would have waved the offer away rather than doing something as intimate as sharing a beverage from the same cup. But he didn't want to make the situation awkward and he had already used his mouth and tongue in other intimate ways with Abe, so instead he reached for the cup, said, "Thanks," and took a sip.

"What do you think?"

"It's good," Jason said as he handed the cup back to Abe. "I'll try it that way next time."

Abe nodded and took the mug. "Did you have a nice Christmas?"

"Yeah. You?"

"Uh-huh. I went to Utah for a few days. Saw my family. It was nice." Abe ran his finger around the rim of his cup and then looked up at Jason from underneath his lashes. "So this is weird, right?"

"No," Jason replied too quickly. When Abe arched his eyebrows, Jason sighed. "Maybe a little."

"I can go."

For a second, Jason considered agreeing. He didn't need a new friend and he could find sex easily without awkward conversations or frequent trips to coffee shops. But then he remembered what his cousin Asher had said about coming home to someone who was thrilled to see him, and he felt a pang of longing for the same thing. Jason not only wanted someone to feel that way about him, he ached with the need to feel the same in return. And the man across the table was the only person who had ever captured his attention long enough to make him want a repeat, let alone a threepeat.

"No, don't go." He reached out and grasped Abe's forearm. "I know I'm not good at this, but I don't want you to leave."

"This?"

"Conversation," Jason clarified.

Grinning, Abe said, "You definitely have an easier time talking when the clothes come off. I'll give you that."

The memory of Abe's lithe body bared of clothing slammed into Jason's brain. His belly tightened and his cock filled.

"Wow." Abe coughed and then cleared his throat. "I've heard the phrase 'undressing someone with your eyes' but I don't think I've ever actually seen it happen until just now."

"Sorry." Jason shrugged unapologetically. "You're hot naked."

"I should probably be offended, but I'm too busy being flattered." Abe paused. "And you're hot naked too." His forehead creased. "That was a really strange round of compliments."

Jason chuckled. "Yes, it was, but thank you."

"So, you need help making conversation. Let's see...." Abe drew in a deep breath. "We've gone over the best way to order chai and our respective naked hotness, so I think the only thing left to talk about now is CrossFit."

"What?"

"CrossFit. It's the big exercise thing everybody's doing. You haven't heard of it?"

"No. But the people I talk to about exercise don't normally give me those types of details." Those people were patients, but Jason didn't yet feel ready to give Abe specific biographical information about himself. There were only so many cardiothoracic surgeons in town, and his occupation combined with his first name and age were enough for Abe to learn a lot more about him.

"That's because they don't do CrossFit," Abe said. "If they did, they'd tell you all about it before they said a single other thing, including hello or their name. It's one of the requirements in their membership contract."

"Really?"

"Seems that way," Abe said with a shrug. "So, no CrossFit. Um, okay, I have another conversation idea." He leaned forward and smiled broadly. "I'll ask a question, and you answer superfast without thinking about what you're going to say. Like, gut responses. Then you do the same to me. Sound good?"

It sounded ridiculous, but Jason didn't have any better ideas, and he liked how Abe's eyes sparkled when he got excited, so he said, "Yes. Sure."

"Cool." Abe pursed his lips in thought. "Three things you enjoy. Go!"

"Uh...."

"No thinking!" he exclaimed.

"I don't know. I, uh—"

"Gut reaction!"

"Fucking, college basketball, and cold pizza," Jason replied hurriedly. He froze after the words popped out of his mouth, surprised by what he'd said. It was true, but not exactly the kind of information he threw out there. Except he had.

Abe was silent for few moments, then he blinked, cleared his throat, and said, "What's your favorite team?"

"Duke."

Abe nodded. "And you like your pizza cold?"

Apparently they were moving forward with the conversation. Okay. "I like it hot too, but, yeah, I like it cold better. I always order extra so I can put it in the fridge for the next day."

"I see." Abe nodded again. "So, uh, do you have plans tonight?"

"No." Jason shook his head.

"Neither do I." Abe glanced down, bit his lip, and then looked up again. "Want to come over and do that first thing you enjoy?"

"Yes," Jason said in relief, and then, worried he had taken a misstep in his goal of getting to know Abe, he added, "I mean, we can talk some more if you want to."

"God, no." Abe shook his head and stood up. "I think we need a break from that. It was exhausting." He smiled, letting Jason know he wasn't upset. "But it's early, so we can try again between rounds."

The turn of events was unexpected but welcome. Very welcome. So Jason quickly rose and followed Abe out of the coffee shop. It seemed he was a better conversationalist than he had realized. Or a worse one. Didn't matter. Either way, he was getting laid.

Chapter 4

ABE WOULDN'T describe himself as completely buttoned-up when
it came to sex, but he wasn't wildly uninhibited either. He'd had two
boyfriends in his twenty-six years, the first shortly after he came out
when he was twenty-one and the next not long after he graduated
from college. Neither relationship had lasted a year, and though he
had slept with both men, it wasn't right away.

Growing up in conservative Salt Lake City, Utah, meant
family values were instilled in him from a young age. Although his
parents' marriage hadn't worked out, both of them had remarried
shortly after their divorce and were still married to his stepparents.
His older sister had married at twenty-two and by all accounts was
very happy. The friends he had grown up with were almost all
married, and their Facebook photos had shifted from couple photos
to baby photos. The bottom line was that Abe was a relationship
guy—born and raised.

Ironically, that aspect of his nature was what had led to the
demise of his relationships. When he realized he wasn't forever
compatible with a man, he no longer saw the point in dating him and
couldn't bring himself to sleep with him. Which was what made his
attraction and reaction to Jason so out of character.

Normally, Abe was a follower when it came to sex. Spending
almost every Sunday of his youth in a church pew had established a
niggling voice in the back of his head that associated sex outside of

marriage with sin. Though he had long since left the church and he was happy with who he was, the echo of the voice still lingered, so it was easier to go along with his boyfriends' suggestions than to take the lead and thereby admit what he wanted.

But things with Jason had been different from the get-go. The rules of their interaction had been established on the first night—they were going to have sex, nothing less and most certainly nothing more. The decision, once made, had been incredibly freeing for Abe. He had already admitted what he wanted to do with Jason. There was no denying it and therefore no reason to shy away from it. Even when the one-night-stand he had justified as a wild deviation from his normal life had turned into a second night, the rules had stayed the same and so had the freedom Abe felt to relish the experience.

When Jason asked him to sit down in the coffee shop that evening, the rules of engagement had shifted. They'd intentionally spent time together with their clothes on. Plus, charmingly awkward though it was, they'd had a conversation, not in order to pass the time in a car ride, but to get to know each other. But regardless of those changes, their method of interaction in the bedroom had already been established, so with Jason, Abe acted without guilt or hesitation.

"I'm glad I ran into you tonight," Jason said.

"Me too." Abe turned the lock on his front door and moaned when Jason pressed up against his back, wrapped his arm around Abe's waist, and mouthed his neck. Abe had barely managed to keep himself in check before they'd gotten to his apartment. Now, all bets were off. He rocked his hips backward, rubbing his ass over Jason's groin. "You feel good," he said when he made contact with the long, hard ridge behind Jason's zipper.

"Going to make you feel even better in a second."

Jason flicked Abe's zipper open and tugged his jeans and briefs down below his backside. He humped against Abe one time, the rough fabric of his pants dragging against Abe's sensitive skin, and then he moved away. Abe snaked his hand behind his back and helped Jason open his button and zipper. Within seconds, Jason was against him again—his chest plastered to Abe's back and his dick rubbing against Abe's cleft. He wound his arms around Abe, tweaking his nipple with one hand and cupping his balls with the other.

"I love your mouth and your hand, baby, but tonight I want to be inside," Jason said as he moved his hand beyond Abe's balls and tickled his fingertips over the wrinkled flesh around his hole. "Are you into that?"

Abe's cock filled, his balls tightened, and his belly clenched in anticipation. His previous experiences with Jason made him associate the verbally reserved but physically demonstrative man with pleasure. They had gone down on each other, stroked each other off, and rubbed off against each other. Abe had enjoyed every second of it. His orgasms had been strong and drawn-out, and the foreplay had been intense and passionate, so now he instinctively reacted with desire to any suggestion involving sex with Jason.

"Yes," he whispered, pressing against Jason's hand.

"Let's go to the bedroom." Jason licked a swath up Abe's neck and nibbled on his ear. "I want you laid out in front of me naked." He moved his hand over Abe's balls and stroked his erection. "Did I already tell you how gorgeous you are?"

"You...." Abe swallowed hard and tipped his head back so he could look at Jason's rugged face. "You said I was hot."

"Mmm. That too." Jason tugged Abe's briefs and jeans up over his hips but left them unfastened. "Let's go," he said as he righted his own pants. He grasped Abe's hand and pulled him across the apartment.

When they reached the bedroom, they both quickly stripped and climbed onto the bed.

"Is your stuff in the nightstand? Once we get started, I don't want to stop again," Jason said. At first Abe didn't understand the question, but then Jason explained. "Condoms? Lube? Are they in the nightstand?"

"Oh." Abe blinked. "Lube, yes, but I don't have any condoms."

He used the lube to get himself off, but his last relationship had ended three apartments and close to three years earlier, and he hadn't had a reason to buy rubbers since. After all, he wasn't the type to jump right into bed with someone he was newly dating.

Although he apparently had no compunction about jumping into bed with someone he *wasn't* dating. The realization made him laugh.

In middle of stretching toward the nightstand, Jason stopped, gazed at Abe, and said, "You have a great laugh."

Hearing Jason compliment his body wasn't a surprise, because from the beginning the sole purpose of their time together had been a mutual desire to explore each other physically. But a compliment about his laugh was something else entirely; it had nothing to do with getting off.

"I, uh…." Abe lowered his gaze and then raised it and chewed on his bottom lip. "Yeah?"

Jason nodded and cupped his cheek. "It was the first thing I noticed about you."

Having always wanted to live a white-picket-fence life with a forever guy meant Abe had a tendency to think about the potential future when other guys were still thinking about whether they wanted to go on a first date. But from the beginning, he had known there would be no future with Jason, so his mind hadn't wandered to fantasies that weren't of the naked-and-sticky variety. That worked fine when all Jason offered was physical affection. But sweet comments and gentle touches were a surefire way to involve Abe's heart, and he wasn't sure how he felt about that. Letting go of his self-imposed bedroom limits didn't impact anything except his orgasm count and his ability to tell himself he'd never had meaningless sex. Getting emotionally involved with a man who had made clear the limitations of his interest to the point where he didn't share even the most basic information, like his last name, had the very real potential of devastating Abe.

"I think I have a condom in my wallet," Jason said, continuing their earlier conversation.

The reminder that Abe was in bed with a man who had casual sex frequently enough to carry a stash of supplies got the interaction back on familiar ground, which was comforting, if a bit disappointing. Abe had enjoyed the focused expression on Jason's face when they chatted, the warmth of Jason's skin as he held his hand, and the softness in Jason's caress. Receiving that tenderness from the same man who turned him on by handling him aggressively and using his body shamelessly was a melding of the qualities Abe openly admitted he wanted in a partner and those he pulled out of hiding only as masturbatory material.

"Be right back." Jason nipped Abe's ear, hopped off the bed, and returned seconds later with a condom packet.

He set it on the pillow before reaching for the nightstand again. Because he was straddling Abe's leg, the motion caused his erection to drag across Abe's hip, which returned Abe's attention to what they were about to do.

"Was that a horny moan or an I'm-squishing-you sound?" Jason asked as he set Abe's tube of K-Y next to the condom. He settled himself between Abe's legs and massaged his thighs, pushing hard against the muscles and dragging his hands up until he brushed Abe's balls with his thumbs.

"Not squishing me," Abe said breathlessly as he spread his legs farther apart.

"Good." Jason continued his firm massage as he lowered his face and blew hot air across Abe's testicles. "You have great nuts." He lapped at Abe's sac. "I love how they hang." He took one testicle into his mouth and suckled. "You're so soft," he mumbled as he released one and then sucked on the other.

"Oh God," Abe groaned. He quickly reached between his legs and buried his fingers in Jason's hair. "Don't stop. Please, I…. Don't stop."

Though Jason didn't verbally respond, he sucked harder, decreased the pressure, licked, and then sucked voraciously again.

Abe threw his head back and closed his eyes, lost in a haze of pleasure. When Jason circled his pucker with slick fingers, his breath hitched. Unable to move or speak, he stayed perfectly still, waiting for what he knew was coming next. It didn't take long for Jason to slowly push one digit into his hole, and Abe cried out, the sound a mixture between a moan and a wail.

"You're really tight, baby. Are you nervous?" Jason rubbed his thumb over Abe's perineum, pressing down against the smooth skin as he pumped his finger in and out of Abe's channel.

"Not nervous," Abe croaked. "It's just been a while."

"How long?" Jason kissed Abe's hip and added another finger.

"Few years."

Jason stopped.

"What's wrong?" Abe blinked and looked down to see Jason's perplexed expression.

"Why so long?" Jason asked. "Don't you like it?"

"I broke up with my last boyfriend about three years ago," Abe explained. Or at least he thought he was explaining. When Jason's expression didn't change, he realized he needed to elaborate. "I haven't met anyone who I connected with enough to get serious, and I don't have sex with random guys or even guys I go out with a few times. That's not who I am."

Jason arched his eyebrows and looked down at Abe's hole, currently filled by two of Jason's fingers, and then returned his gaze to Abe.

"This is an anomaly," Abe said.

"Is that right?" Jason smirked as he slowly withdrew his fingers and then slid them back in, his gaze never leaving Abe's face.

Abe opened his mouth, but when Jason brushed over his gland, a gasp came out instead of words. He swallowed down the thickness in his throat and then rasped, "Yes."

"I like the sound of that." Jason pushed in again and tapped against Abe's gland a couple of times before pulling out. "Makes me feel like I'm irresistible."

Abe chuckled, the sound strained because he was barely breathing. "And arrogant," he said.

"That too." Jason twisted his fingers. "You're so hot inside, so smooth." He worked Abe over until liquid dripped from his slit, and then he leaned forward and licked it up. "Mmm."

"That's so sexy." Abe gulped. His groin clenched and his dick throbbed. "I'm already close."

"Yeah?" Jason thrust his fingers in and out quickly, grazing Abe's prostate on every stroke. "How close?"

"Are you trying to torture me?"

Jason's eyes twinkled and lines formed at the corners as he grinned. "Uh-huh. But it's the good kind."

"There's a good kind of torture?" Abe asked, dragging in a breath between each word.

"You tell me." Jason wrapped his free hand around Abe's cock and started stroking while he pegged Abe's gland.

"Ah!" Abe bucked, thrusting his hips up.

"Well?"

Barely able to suck in enough air to breathe, let alone answer questions, Abe panted and stared at Jason.

"Good, right?" He twisted his hand around Abe's crown and tilted one side of his mouth up.

"Yes. Good." Abe rocked his hips up and down in concert with Jason's motions. "Good but evil."

Jason chuckled and crawled up Abe's torso. He rubbed his hands up and down Abe's flanks. "You're fun," he said.

Smiling broadly, Abe traced one of Jason's dark eyebrows with his finger. "So are you."

"I want to do this again," Jason admitted quietly.

"I want to do it the first time," Abe responded.

Jason snorted. "Fair enough." He reached for the condom packet, opened it, and then rolled the condom over his rigid, dark brown shaft. He popped open the lube, slicked himself, and then tossed it aside. "Let's see if I can earn myself an invitation for a repeat performance."

"I'll let you know if you pass muster."

Chuckling, Jason said, "You do that."

He grasped Abe's thighs and lifted them up and out, opening Abe to his view. Then he lined himself up with Abe's hole and circled his hips, dragging his cockhead across the sensitive skin.

"Ah," Abe groaned.

Jason held on to one of Abe's legs and wrapped the other around his back. He gripped his own cock and pushed his glans against Abe's pucker and then slowly sank inside. "Christ," Jason hissed. "You feel so damn good."

Abe tilted his ass up, giving Jason an easier angle. "More," he said. He clutched Jason's arms and looked at his face, tight with concentration. "Give me more. I want it."

Jason pulled back an inch and then slammed in to the hilt. Abe opened his mouth on a soundless wail, but he didn't push Jason away. Instead, he held on tighter and arched his back, trying to get as close as possible.

"Yes," Jason said. He pulled out quickly and shoved back in even faster, taking Abe hard, pumping in and out again and again.

Relishing having his channel stretched and filled and his gland massaged by Jason's thick cock, Abe grunted and humped up, meeting every stroke. There was nothing else like this. Not his own fingers and not even the toy he had once been brave enough to try. The heat, the hardness with enough give to make the glide comfortable, the full mushroom cap as it popped out and then penetrated him again—all of it drove Abe to the edge.

Crying out, Abe planted both feet on the bed and pushed himself up. He slapped hard against Jason and gasped. "Don't stop," he said as he thrust up and down. "Please don't stop."

"That's it, baby," Jason said hoarsely. "Work yourself off on me." Clumsily, Jason reached for Abe's hands. He pressed them against the mattress on either side of Abe's shoulders, twined their fingers together, and gazed at Abe's face as he pumped harder and faster, his hairy belly rubbing against Abe's cock.

Both of them gasped for air as they slammed their overheated bodies together, taking and giving as they raced to completion.

"I'm there. I'm there. I'm there," Abe said as his muscles tightened up. "Jase!" He arched and came, shooting hot seed between them.

As if in response to Abe's release, Jason pushed in deep, held still, and groaned as his cock pulsed. He gazed into Abe's eyes as he came, the moment so painfully intimate that Abe knew he'd never be able to describe what they'd shared as *just* a hookup.

When Jason stopped twitching, he leaned forward and pressed his mouth to Abe's. The first kiss was tentative, but then Abe parted his lips, Jason slipped his tongue inside, and both of them moaned. Jason cupped both sides of Abe's face as he slanted his mouth over Abe's and twined their tongues together. Abe writhed underneath him, grasping his wrists and sucking on his tongue.

After a few minutes, Jason pulled away. "Damn," he said breathlessly. He tugged Abe's bottom lip between his teeth, licked it, and then smiled. "You're a good kisser."

"We can do it again," Abe said, his heart pounding.

"Give me a second to clean us up." Jason reached between them and held on to the condom as he pulled out. Abe shuddered at the loss and Jason gently smiled at him.

"You're really cute."

"Thanks."

"Makes me want to fuck you again."

"Charming," Abe said, laughing.

Jason waggled his eyebrows and started climbing out of bed.

"You're coming back, right?" Abe asked as he grabbed Jason's hand.

"Yeah, baby." Jason lifted their joined hands and kissed the back of Abe's. "It's still early." He licked Abe's wrist. "I'm not done with you yet."

Jason walked out of the room and Abe mumbled, "You're going to kill me."

The toilet flushed, and then Jason yelled out, "How's your heart?" as the water in the sink started running.

"Uh, good, I guess. Other than my asthma, my physicals are always clear. Why?"

"Just wanted to make sure we won't have any death by orgasms on my watch," Jason said as he returned. He climbed onto the bed and wiped the semen off Abe with a warm washcloth.

The act was so thoughtful, Abe's heart clenched.

"I'll make sure not to chase you around the room so fast you lose your breath," Jason said as he tossed the washcloth aside. "That should keep us in the clear."

"Thanks," Abe whispered.

Jason lay down next to him. He traced Abe's nipple with one hand and propped his head up on the other. "So. What do you want to do while we recharge?"

Abe scooted closer until their bodies were pressed together. "We could finish the game from earlier. I think it's your turn to ask questions."

"Sounds good." Jason reached up and combed his fingers through Abe's hair. "Did I prove myself enough to get a return invite?"

"Do you want to come back?" Abe asked, not sure what answer he wanted to hear. He'd be sad if Jason said no and walked out of his life. But if they spent too much time together, the inevitable end would hurt even more.

"Yeah," Jason said softly, his expression a mixture of perplexed and happy. "I'm pretty sure I do."

Chapter 5

NORMALLY WHEN the orgasm was over, Jason was itching to leave whomever he was with. But after two leg-numbing rounds with Abe, he hadn't been ready to say good night. He stayed in bed, his arm wrapped around Abe's shoulders and Abe's head pillowed on his chest, and chatted with him about nothing until Abe fell asleep. Though he didn't see himself getting serious enough about a man to live with him, like his cousin Asher had done, Jason couldn't deny how much he enjoyed being with Abe.

The screwing was obviously and predictably good. The interesting and amusing conversations were somewhat unexpected but not a huge surprise considering Abe's vibrant, if a bit shy, personality and Jason's lack of human interaction outside of work. But it was the deep-seated satisfaction he felt when he held Abe in his arms that stunned Jason.

Was he so starved for physical affection that he suddenly enjoyed being in bed with someone with no purpose or goal? That didn't make sense, because despite being single, Jason had an active sex life. He had always had a high sex drive. During his marriage, he had tried to keep it in check, tried to remain faithful, and failed more frequently than he succeeded. After Angela left him, he figured there was nothing holding him back. Though he couldn't have most of what he'd hoped for in life, the benefit of divorce meant he could get laid whenever he wanted, and it was a benefit he took advantage of whenever he had free time. His physical needs were being met several times a week, so horniness wasn't an explanation.

With no excuse coming to mind, Jason decided not to worry about it. Abe clearly enjoyed lying in bed with him even after they were done fucking, so nobody was being put out. More importantly, Abe said he was interested in getting together again, which meant Jason had accomplished his goal for the night. He didn't know how long it'd last, but for now, he'd try some version of what his cousin Asher had suggested—fucking the same guy repeatedly.

Yawning, Jason realized he had to get up and go home before he fell asleep. He slid out of bed carefully so he wouldn't wake Abe and then pulled the blanket over his pale, wiry body. After dressing quickly, he walked back to the side of the bed and gazed down at Abe again, the security lights outside illuminating Abe's face.

Abe's body was lean but his face was round and his cheeks plump. Those features, combined with his scruffy blond hair and his huge blue eyes, lent him an air of innocence. And though Abe was uninhibited and voracious in bed, he didn't have a lot of experience, so Jason's perception wasn't far from the mark. But instead of making him want to escape and spend his time with men like himself—men who knew what they were doing and weren't likely to get emotionally involved, men who had lived enough to understand the score, men who knew from personal experience how to make him feel good without involving any feelings—Jason found he enjoyed being graced with the hopeful and trusting glances the younger man hadn't yet learned to shield. A pang in his chest accompanied a flash of need to protect Abe from having those traits dashed.

Shaking his head at the fanciful thought, Jason pulled an old receipt from his wallet, looked around for a pen, and then jotted down a quick note: *Thanks for tonight. Call me if you want to do it again.* He added his number to the bottom and tucked the paper under Abe's phone, where he knew Abe would find it. Then he left the apartment and drove home to get some sleep. He was on call for the next week; he needed the rest.

"ANGELA?" JASON said when his ex-wife answered the phone. "I got your message. What's going on?"

Jason had been working almost nonstop all week, going home to crash and grab a change of clothes and then returning to the hospital the next morning. With that schedule, he hadn't had time or energy to return calls, but one of the receptionists on the cardiology wing had come to him with an urgent message, so he dialed up his ex to see what she needed.

"I want to make sure you remember we're meeting with Kristen's teacher today at four."

"What?"

"Kristen's math teacher. We scheduled the appointment in November but you had to miss it, so I rescheduled, but you had a last-minute conflict again, so I switched it to after the semester break. It's today at four. Do you need the address?"

"I know where Kristen goes to school," Jason grumbled.

"Fine."

"I realize I haven't been there, but she's in high school now. It's not as if parents just stop by."

"I only wanted to make sure you were set for the meeting, Jason."

"And she takes the school bus or gets rides with her friends. Why would I go there?"

Angela sighed. "Well, today you'll be going there to meet with her math teacher. At four."

"I've had a long week, Ange. I'm not sure I—"

"No."

"Excuse me?" Jason said.

"You heard me. I said no. Our daughter's teacher wants to meet with us, and our daughter asked both of us to attend. She doesn't ask for much. We will both be there."

"Fine. I'm not saying I won't go. But today isn't good. Like I said, I've been working all week, and I'm beat."

And high-strung and uptight and grouchy. This was the way he'd felt when he was married and trying to stay faithful to his wife.

It was also the reason he'd sought sex elsewhere and justified it by telling himself it made him a better husband and father because getting off released his tension. After the week he'd had, a good, hard fuck was what he needed, not a school meeting.

"We cannot put this off again, Jason. Kristen's teacher wanted to meet with us before the end of the semester. We're already late. I don't want to keep dragging this out and I checked with your scheduler. I know you're off at three today. That gives you enough time to wash up and get to the school."

"You talked to Tina?"

"Yes."

"I can't believe she told you my schedule."

"I delivered both of her children."

Right. He had forgotten. Angela was considered one of the best ob-gyns in town, and getting in to see her was almost impossible because her practice was closed to new patients. But she was willing to open new slots for friends, which included Jason's employees and their wives.

"You said four?"

"Yes. In room A34. Do you want to meet in front of the school or do you know where the A building is?"

"I think I can locate a classroom." Jason furrowed his brow and tried to decide if he was being overly sensitive. The answer was probably yes because Angela wasn't the type to be intentionally mean, even when it was warranted. Jason knew that firsthand. "I'll meet you there," he said more calmly.

"Thanks, Jason."

Angela shouldn't have to thank him for attending a meeting about his daughter, one of the few things Kristen had ever asked him to do. He dragged his fingers through his hair and sighed. "No, thank you," he said sincerely. "I appreciate you reminding me. I would have forgotten."

"No problem." Angela paused but didn't hang up, so he knew she wanted to say something else.

"What?" he asked.

"If you're not busy after the meeting, I'm sure Kristen would love to go out to dinner with you. She's planning to go to the basketball game at the school, but that doesn't start until seven, so there'll be time for you to grab a bite in between. I'll be picking up Donny, so it'd be just the two of you."

When had he last spent one-on-one time with his daughter? Jason couldn't remember, which meant it had been too long. And an early dinner wouldn't impede on his plans for the night.

Jason's nerves were wound tight and his skin felt too stretched. Abe had left him a message a few days earlier, and Jason had been planning to call him back when he finished his shift. He was good for a few hard fucks and hoped Abe was free that night so he could stop by and burn off some tension between the sheets. He also hoped Abe didn't have plans the next morning, because Jason wasn't scheduled to work all weekend and the thought of sleeping with Abe in his arms again made his belly warm and his chest ache.

"Dinner sounds good," he said. "Should I drop her back at the school when we're done?"

"Yes. She's spending the night at Ilia's, so her mother will take them home after the game."

Jason didn't know who Ilia was, but he assumed she was one of his daughter's friends. "Okay," he said. "I'll see you at the school in a few hours."

JASON ARRIVED at his daughter's school on time—five minutes after four was close enough to the meeting time to count, just like going five miles over the speed limit was close enough not to result in a speeding ticket. Unfortunately, the school campus was larger than he had anticipated, and the buildings weren't arranged in any obvious order. He double-checked the text Angela had sent him with the room number and once again saw that it was A34. After making another lap around the school, he finally came upon the A building all the way in the back corner.

His phone rang at that moment, and he notice the time when he looked at the screen.

"I'm about to walk in, Ange," he said as he stomped toward the door. "It's not even a quarter after yet." He grabbed the doorknob and turned it as he pulled. "And I can't be held responsible for the flawed design of this school. How can you trust these people to educate our daughter if they don't understand the order of the alphabet?"

"There he is now," Angela said.

It took Jason a moment to realize her voice wasn't coming from the phone. He glanced up and saw Angela, Kristen, and a man whose back was to Jason sitting around a triangle-shaped table. A half-dozen of them filled the room instead of desks. He would have worked up some sort of barb about the new learning environment, but his daughter spoke first.

"Mr. Green, this is my father, Dr. Garcia," she said. "Dad, this is Mr. Green."

The teacher stood up and turned around to welcome him. The warm blue eyes and free smile were already familiar, but they left the moment Abe laid eyes on Jason, replaced by wide eyes and a furrowed brow. Jason much preferred a sleepy, sated Abe or a mindlessly aroused Abe, or even a laughing, teasing Abe to this concerned, confused version.

"Your father?" Abe said, his voice scratchy.

"Jason Garcia," Jason said, forcing himself to step forward and reach his hand out for a shake instead of pulling Abe into his arms and kissing away that worried expression. His family was in the room. This was no place to act on his predilections. "It's nice meeting you."

Abe's jaw dropped, and he blinked at an unusually rapid clip. He didn't react to Jason's raised hand.

"I'm sorry I'm late," Jason said as a peace offering.

"Mr. Green?" Kristen said. "Is everything okay? You look a little pale."

Jason didn't correct his daughter by saying that Abe's porcelain skin always gave him that appearance and that he was beautiful, especially when he was naked and tangled with Jason's own dark body. Upon closer inspection, though, Jason realized Kristen was right: Abe did look a little pale. Immediately, Jason dropped his gaze to Abe's chest and tried to count his breaths per minute.

"I'm fine, Kris, thank you." Abe swallowed hard. "Ja—Dr. Garcia, please have a seat." He raised a trembling hand toward Angela. "There's a chair next to your wife."

"Dad," Kristen said. "We're already late." She was tapping her foot on the floor in a gesture that seemed more nervous than frustrated. "Mr. Green was about to get started explaining why we're here."

He wasn't gasping or breathing hard, so Jason dipped his chin in agreement, pulled out the nearest empty chair, and sat down. "Go ahead."

"Th... thank you." Abe returned to his seat and opened a manila folder. "I'm glad you coul—" The papers spilled to the ground, no doubt because of Abe's shaking hands.

"I'll get them, Mr. Green," Angela said. She leaned down, then sat back up and held the papers out to Abe, who was frozen, staring at her hand. "Mr. Green?"

"Sorry," he said. He closed his eyes and shook his head again. "Sorry." He drew in a deep breath and opened his eyes. "There should be a copy there for each of you," he said to Angela. "Please go ahead and pass them around."

"What is this?" Jason said when he looked at the paper Angela handed him.

"Kris's results from the assessments we gave the kids. The first column shows Kris's scores from the first week of school, the second one shows the scores from an assessment in mid-October, and the third one shows the scores from one she got on Monday."

There were four columns, one blank and three with numbers, but Jason had no context to understand what they meant.

"Is Kristen having trouble in school?" Angela asked, her gaze darting between Abe and Kristen.

"No, not at all." Abe's voice sounded steadier, stronger.

Jason's shoulders eased in response. He had hated seeing the other man so clearly upset.

"In fact," Abe went on, "she's doing exceptionally well." He looked at Kristen and smiled. Her cheeks colored and she lowered her gaze and stared at the table. "The math score you see for the beginning of the year is what we'd expect from sophomores at the end of the year. That means Kris started out the year essentially two grade levels ahead. We talked about it, and she decided to work on a specialized lesson plan."

"A specialized lesson plan?" Angela asked.

"I came in after school and Mr. Green taught me. He made lesson plans especially for me," Kristen said excitedly, her words rushed. "And then in class, I did the work he gave me while he taught the regular lesson. He even let me come in during winter break for a lesson and gave me extra work to do at home."

Abe laughed, the sound a balm to Jason's frayed nerves. The entire interaction had him on edge. He felt like he was waging a battle inside himself and he had no idea why, over what, or what side he was on.

"I have never had a student who was so excited about doing extra work." Abe shook his head and smiled at Kris again. She beamed.

"You've been meeting with my daughter after school hours and on vacation?" Angela asked, her voice slow and low. That was never a good sign.

"Mom!" Kristen shouted. "It wasn't like that!"

Like what? Jason wondered. He looked at Angela and saw her dangerous expression focused on Abe. Oh, Lord. Did she actually think the man was behaving inappropriately with their daughter? Couldn't she tell Abe was way too sweet, too earnest, and too damn gay to ever do such a thing?

"Mr. Green has been helping me. He says I have great potential!"

"He does, does he?" Angela said, her tone biting and sarcastic. *"Potential?"*

How she managed to make the word sound dirty, he didn't know, but she did. And though Jason didn't want to expose what he did in his personal time to his family, he couldn't let Abe fall victim to anger or accusations. His stomach rolled at the stricken expression on the face he'd been longing to see and touch for days, and the need to protect Abe outweighed everything else.

"Ange," Jason hissed and clasped her hand. "Tone it down and let the man speak. They've been doing algebra, for Christ's sake, not reading romantic poetry."

"Calculus, actually," Abe corrected shakily. "We got through geometry and trigonometry last semester, and now we're working on calculus. If you look at the test scores from Monday, you'll see that Kris is now at the level of a first-semester twelfth grader."

That information banked Angela's fire. "Really?" She darted her gaze from the paper to Kristen. "That's wonderful."

"Thanks, Mom." Kristen smiled at her mother and then looked at Jason expectantly.

"That's really good, Kristen. It sounds like you're working hard."

"She has been," Abe said. "And she wants to keep it up, which is why we asked for this meeting."

"We?" Angela asked.

"Kris and I," Abe responded. "My students are old enough to take responsibility for their education decisions." He patted Kristen's shoulder. "Some do it better than others. And in Kris's case, she wants to take classes at the community college."

"What kind of classes?" Angela asked.

"You're only fourteen," Jason said.

"Fifteen," Kristen and Angela said in unison.

Her birthday had been on December 11, less than a month earlier, so he was practically right, but he didn't bother arguing.

"I talked with the principal, and we are in agreement that the school will support Kris if she wants to move faster than we're able to accomplish. She can take study hall during her math hour, so she'll have time to do homework during the day to make up for the time she'll spend in her community college class after school hours. And we can give her credit for the college course toward her graduation requirements here."

Jason looked at Angela, his eyebrows arched questioningly. The idea sounded good to him. If Kristen wanted to work harder and earn college credit early, he saw no reason to stand in her way.

"We'll have to think about it and look at the schedule to make sure there are classes available after school hours," Angela said.

"I already looked, Mom," Kris said. "There's a calculus class this semester at the CSN Henderson campus. Tuesdays and Thursdays from four thirty to six fifteen." She bit her lip and tapped her foot. "Please?"

Jason didn't remember ever being that excited about school. He had excelled, but that was because academics came easily to him and he wanted to rank higher than his classmates, not because he enjoyed doing the work.

"We need to think about this, Kristen," Angela said. "Your father and I both work, so we'll have to see if there's a way to get you to class."

"I can take the city bus to class and then you can pick me up after work," she said to her mother. "You're usually home right around that time."

"No, you cannot take the city bus," Jason growled. He might not interfere much when it came to parenting, but his little girl was not getting on a bus filled with strangers. Adult strangers. *Male* adult strangers. He knew exactly what they'd think when they got a look at her.

Abe chuckled, stealing Jason's attention. He darted his gaze to Abe's smiling face and immediately wanted to shove his cock between those plump red lips and tangle his fingers in the disheveled blond hair while those big blue eyes looked up at him. Yes, it was safe to say he had an excellent idea of how the male mind worked, and it was not getting access to his daughter.

"You're too young to go riding all around town on the bus," Jason said.

"It's not all around town! The campus isn't far."

"You heard your father," Angela said. "This time next year you'll have your driver's license and we can reevaluate."

"It's not fair!" Kristen yelled as she shot out of her chair. "This is the one thing I'm good at! The one thing that makes me feel... makes me feel.... It makes sense, and when I'm doing it my head makes sense, and you won't even let me try!" In an unusual-for-her moment of drama, she raced out of the room.

All three of them looked at the door in shock for a few moments and then refocused on each other.

"Well." Angela cleared her throat. "I apologize for that display. Kristen is usually much more even-keeled. I don't know what got into her."

"She genuinely enjoys learning," Abe said. "I know she was hoping you'd let her take the calculus course, so she's probably disappointed." He reached for the papers strewn across the table and chewed on his upper lip. "I realize your family has a lot to consider, but if the only issue is transportation"—he raised his gaze to Angela and then flicked it to Jason—"I'm happy to drive her there. It's not far and I have the time."

"Why would you do that?" Angela asked suspiciously. "What would you get out of it?"

Abe flinched and his expression fell. "I'm sorry. I was only trying to help." He got up. "I can see it wasn't a good idea." He wiped his hands on his khakis, drawing Jason's attention to them and making him realize Abe was trembling again.

"Abe," he said, reaching his hand out as he stood. "We didn't mean anything by that." Abe moved forward to pick up the manila folder, and Jason grabbed hold of his wrist. He held on tightly enough to keep Abe in place, but not hard enough to bruise. "We know you're offering your time because you want to help Kristen." He looked at Angela while he subconsciously rubbed his thumb back and forth across Abe's wrist, trying to soothe. "Isn't that right, Angela?"

Angela opened her mouth and then paused as she darted her gaze back and forth between Jason and Abe. "Right," she said slowly. She lowered her gaze, wrinkled her forehead in thought, and then cleared her throat. "That's right," she said, her tone completely changed. "We would very much appreciate the help, Mr. Green." She smiled at Abe as she stood up. "Please let us know if you need us to compensate you for gas money or travel time."

Jason squeezed Abe's wrist before releasing him. He beamed at Angela, thrilled she'd finally seen the good in Abe.

"Th... that won't be necessary," Abe said, looking back and forth between Jason and Angela, no doubt confused about the sudden change in attitude. "Like I said, CSN Henderson isn't far, and I have the time."

"Thanks, Abe," Jason said. He reached his hand out again, but Abe stepped back. With the table between them, Jason could no longer reach him, which bothered him unreasonably. "Is everything okay?" he asked.

"Everything is fine," Abe said, his voice stilted. He jerked his gaze toward Angela and then returned it to Jason. "I'm sure Kris will want to hear the good news. I'll let you go so she isn't kept waiting." He tipped his chin toward the door. "Thank you both for making the time for this meeting."

Chapter 6

ABE WAS rinsing out his soup bowl when his doorbell rang. "Just a minute," he called out as he turned off the faucet. He grabbed a towel, dried his hands, and tossed it onto the counter before walking toward the front door. "What can I do for—" He froze midsentence when he opened the door and came face-to-face with Jason. He couldn't help the needy lurch in his belly or the tingling across his skin as he remembered how good Jason's touch had felt. "What are you doing here?" he said, his voice strained.

"I'm not that early, am I?" Jason asked. He pulled his phone out of his pocket, glanced at it, and then looked back at Abe. "It's a quarter after seven and we said seven thirty."

Abe gaped at him for several seconds and then gathered his mental faculties, such as they were after that afternoon's fiasco, and said, "*We* didn't say anything. I left you a message three days ago and I didn't hear word one from you until you sent me a text this afternoon while I was working announcing that you were coming over at seven thirty."

"I've been at the hospital all week. One doctor in our group is on vacation and another has the flu, so we were scrambling. I got in touch with you as soon as I was off work."

The conversation was surreal. Abe stared at Jason, waiting for him to acknowledge the other issue, the one that mattered more than how long it took him to respond to Abe's call or how arrogant and rude it was to assume he could text that afternoon, have Abe drop everything to see him, and then, without Abe's agreement, show up on his doorstep uninvited.

When Jason didn't say anything else, Abe threw his hands up and said, "That was before I met your *wife*. I'd say that kind of thing is a pretty obvious game changer."

"Look, I know Angela was a little rough at first, but she warmed up at the end." Jason put his hand on Abe's shoulder and gave him a gentle squeeze.

Abe's jaw dropped again. He rolled his shoulder, dislodging Jason's hand. Did Jason actually think his wife's demeanor was the issue?

"I get that you're upset about how she acted during the meeting, but can we talk about this inside?" Jason asked.

Yes, apparently that was exactly what he thought. "That's not what I meant," Abe said.

Jason stepped forward and squeezed his large frame between Abe and the doorway. With Abe's surprise at the situation and Jason's strength and bulk, he was able to walk right in.

"I know I said we could grab a bite, but do you mind if we stay in instead? I've had a long day and I want to relax."

Though he wasn't normally one to yell, Abe lost his patience. "You've had a long day?" he said, raising his voice.

"A long week, actually." Jason rubbed his fingers over his temples, bringing Abe's attention to his eyes.

They did look a little red, and there were dark circles under them. Abe had instinctively begun to reach for Jason, wanting to stroke his cheek and ease his tension, when he realized what he was doing and stopped himself. "I'm sorry you had a hard week, but I need you to leave." He crossed his arms over his chest and tucked his hands under his arms to prevent them from visibly shaking. "Please."

"Leave?" Jason said disbelievingly. "But we have plans."

"We don't have plans!" Abe threw his hands up again. "You texted me out of nowhere, announced that we were getting together the same night without asking if I was free, and then showed up even though I didn't respond. It's Friday night. What if I was already busy?"

Jason knit his eyebrows together, ran his gaze up and down Abe's body, and then said, "Are you busy?"

He should say yes, but he didn't like lying, not even white lies. "No. But that isn't the point."

His expression softening, Jason stepped closer. "I have no idea what we're talking about but I have to tell you, you look really great tonight."

"We're talking about…." Abe glanced down at his clothes and then looked at Jason in confusion. "I'm wearing my oldest jeans and a swim-a-thon T-shirt."

"I know." Jason wrapped his arm around Abe's waist and tugged him close. "But you look really cute in it." He rested his cheek on Abe's head. "I've been looking forward to seeing you again all week."

Abe told himself to get away from Jason's hold, not to let a married man be that close to him, but then Jason caressed his cheek and smiled softly at him, and he couldn't make his legs move. "Please don't do this," he whispered as he lowered his gaze in shame.

"Do what?" Jason asked.

"Touch me."

"Why not?" When Abe didn't respond, Jason held his chin between his thumb and his finger and raised his face until their gazes met. "Why don't you want me to touch you? We had a great time together, didn't we?"

They had. In fact, Abe hadn't been able to stop thinking about Jason. About how safe he felt blanketed by his large body, about how his breath caught when he was gifted with a smile or a compliment, about how hard Jason had tried to talk to him and get to know him. Yes, he'd had a great time. Too great.

"Abe?" Jason said, his voice wavering and his eyebrows drawn together in concern. "Did I hurt you?" He skimmed his hand over Abe's back down to his ass and gently rubbed. "I know I was a little rough, but I didn't realize—"

"You didn't hurt me," Abe said. "But that isn't the point." He forced himself to wriggle out of Jason's hold and put space between them. "I realize you said all along that this was just about sex and fun, and I thought I could do that, thought I could be that guy for one night and then another and then—" Abe sighed. "Well, you know. But if being *that guy* means cheating on someone's wife, it isn't for me. Period." He rubbed his palms over his eyes. "It's probably not for me anyway, but your wife, your daughter...." His throat burned and he shook his head. "I'm sick about what we did. You need to leave and never come back."

"Aw, baby, come here." Jason stepped toward him.

Jason hadn't used an endearment with him outside of bed, and it made Abe's chest ache with longing. But he managed to keep his feet rooted to the floor instead of falling into Jason's arms.

"I'm divorced." Jason twined his arm around Abe's shoulder, clasped the back of his neck, and tugged him into a hug. "Angela's the only wife I ever had, so I'm used to hearing her referred to that way. That's why I didn't correct you. It never dawned on me that you thought I was still married."

"Divorced?" Abe looked up at him, searching his dark brown eyes.

Nodding, Jason said, "Five years ago."

"But she was wearing a ring. I saw the ring."

"She loves jewelry and she has tons of it, but she doesn't get to wear much of it at work, so she tends to put it on afterward."

"It wasn't a wedding ring?"

"Not her wedding ring," Jason said with certainty. "It might be one of her grandmother's wedding rings, or it could be something she bought for herself." He met Abe's gaze. "I'm not married."

It wasn't until Jason covered Abe's hand with his own that Abe realized he was clutching Jason's shirt. "So you weren't cheating on her?" Abe said, repeating the information to himself more than asking the question.

Jason flinched. "Not with you, no."

There was background behind that answer, but Abe didn't know if he was in a position to ask about it, so he let it go. Relieved that he could let himself enjoy the scent of Jason's skin and strength of his body, he leaned forward, buried his face against Jason's neck, and inhaled deeply.

"Are you smelling me?" Jason asked as he ran his fingers up Abe's neck, through his hair, and massaged the back of his head.

"Sorry," Abe mumbled. "That's weird, huh?"

"Maybe." Jason lowered his hands to Abe's butt, grabbed both cheeks, and tugged Abe forward and up. "But it turns me on knowing you like how I smell." He circled his hips, dragging his erection across Abe's belly. "Makes me hard."

With a moan, Abe hooked one leg around Jason's thigh and started rocking forward, looking for friction. He needed to stop, not to encourage Jason further. Divorced was infinitely better than married, but there was still the matter of Abe's inability to remain emotionally detached from Jason. Maybe if they had left it at one night, or even two, but now it was too late. He liked Jason and not only in bed. So much so that when he had mistakenly thought Jason was married, his feet had been knocked out from under him, and it had taken every ounce of strength he had to stay upright and not break down on the spot. Only the knowledge that he was at work and his student was in the room had kept Abe together.

"We should stop," Abe said, but his body was in control rather than his brain, so he pressed closer instead of moving away.

"You don't want to stop." Jason dipped down and kissed Abe, the brush of lips gentle at first, but then he moaned and started biting and licking. "It's nuts how much I want you." He slammed his mouth over Abe's, sucked on Abe's tongue, and then thrust his tongue inside Abe's mouth. "Hated seeing you so upset."

"You did?"

"Yes, baby."

Once again, Abe melted in reaction to the endearment. It made him feel like he mattered to Jason, like he was special, like he wasn't just a convenient bed partner.

"You have the best smile, and your laugh…." Jason swallowed hard and shook his head. "You should never be sad." He kissed Abe tenderly. "Not ever."

The chemistry between them burned hot and bright, but it wasn't about sex, or at least not only about sex. It wasn't. Whatever

Jason had said originally, whatever they had both agreed to, things had changed, and not just on Abe's side. He was sure about that even though they hadn't talked about it. He was sure.

"I'm not sad right now." Abe looked into Jason's eyes and whispered, "I'm happy."

"That's good, baby," Jason gazed into Abe's eyes. "I'm really glad. How about horny?" He lifted Abe up, and Abe automatically curled his arms and legs around Jason's thick frame and clung tightly. "Are you horny? Because I want you so bad, I hurt with it."

"I thought you were tired," Abe teased.

"Fuck being tired. You drive me crazy." He bit Abe's lip again and then pushed his tongue into Abe's mouth and thrust in and out frantically. "Never wanted anyone like this."

Abe whimpered and opened himself to Jason's assault, submitting to his passion and need and reveling in it.

"I'm taking you to bed," Jason growled.

"The couch is closer," Abe said breathlessly, his balls already aching.

With a nod, Jason shuffled toward the couch, not releasing his hold on Abe. He nipped his way across Abe's jaw and dug his fingers into Abe's ass in a deep massage.

"I'm not going to last," Abe admitted when Jason dipped one of his fingers into Abe's crack. Even with the fabric barrier, the sensation made his groin tighten.

"That's okay." Jason plopped onto the couch, keeping Abe with him so he was straddling Jason's hips. "We have all night." He reached for the buttons on Abe's jeans and opened them with one tug. "Commando?" He looked at Abe and arched his eyebrows. "Since when do you go commando?"

Abe's belly warmed at the comment. It was yet another reminder that Jason knew him. Admittedly, it wasn't the traditional type of knowledge, not the type of thing he normally discussed with men he was dating, but it was confirmation that they were building a foundation, however unusual the process.

"I don't, usually," Abe confirmed. "But these jeans are so old they're softer than sweats, and there's no zipper, so...." He stopped talking, a bit embarrassed about finishing that sentence.

"You like the way they feel on your dick?" Jason rubbed his palms up Abe's jeans-clad thighs. "You like hanging loose in there and jostling against the fabric?"

With his neck heating, Abe nodded.

"You want to know what I think?" Jason took hold of the bottom of Abe's T-shirt, yanked it off, and then tossed it aside. "I think for as innocent as you are." He kissed Abe's nose. "As sweet." He unbuttoned the top couple of buttons on his own shirt and then pulled off. "Down deep, you want it." He licked Abe's lips. "You need it." He grazed his mouth across Abe's jaw. "You crave it." He swirled his tongue around Abe's earlobe and gently suckled it.

Staring at Jason, Abe panted and tried to catch his breath. He didn't know what Jason meant, but he was incredibly aroused by the tenor of his voice, the heat in his eyes, and the seductiveness of his touch.

"It?" Abe asked shakily.

"Sex." Jason wrapped his big hand around Abe's erection and started stroking slowly. "Being taken and tasted and touched."

There was no denying how much he enjoyed being with Jason in the way he described, but that aside, Abe's sex life had been fairly tame and not particularly frequent. "I don't mess around, and I've only had a couple of boyfriends," he said.

"I remember you telling me that." Jason rubbed his thumb across the head of Abe's cock, and he trembled. "But seeing you like this, I have a hard time imagining you going without." He cupped Abe's balls and rolled them.

"Jase!" Abe grabbed Jason's shoulders and bucked. Nobody had ever talked to him that way. Nobody would have thought he'd want it. But he did. Just like Jason said. He craved it. "Please."

"Look at you." Jason increased the pace of his strokes, gently squeezed Abe's balls, and leaned forward until his mouth was right next to Abe's ear. "You're gagging for it, aren't you?"

With an anguished shout, Abe rose to his knees and humped into Jason's fist. He began shooting on the second stroke, and Jason kept up his pace, working him through the pleasure, making it go on and on until Abe collapsed onto his muscular thighs.

"My God." Abe looked at Jason in awe, his vision blurry from the intensity of his orgasm. "That was…. Oh my God."

"That was sexy as hell," Jason said roughly, his voice like sandpaper. He reached between them, tore his pants open, and raised his hips while he pushed his pants down to midthigh, along with his briefs. His thick cock popped up and slapped against his belly. "Do you see what you do to me?" He began jacking himself. "You're so beautiful when you cum. Look how hard I am because of you."

Abe looked down and whimpered in arousal at the sight of Jason tugging on his hard dick, his strokes rough and fast.

"Watch me," Jason hissed. "You do this to me." He pressed the base of his hand against his balls on the downstroke and then pulled his fist up. "You make me want, make me ache."

With his gaze glued to the erotic display before him, Abe rubbed his palms across Jason's chest and circled his thumbs over Jason's nipples. Jason shuddered, telling Abe without words that he enjoyed the attention.

"You like that?" Abe whispered.

"I like everything you do to me." Jason dropped his forehead against Abe's, both of them looking down as Jason brought himself to the edge. "Twist them, baby."

Abe pinched the brown disks between his thumb and his finger and then turned his hands to the sides.

"Ah!" Jason shouted as the first rope of ejaculate flew from his slit. "Yes, fuck, Abe!"

Abe watched, fascinated as Jason's seed streaked across their stomachs and chests. While Jason trembled with aftershocks, his hand still wrapped around his spent dick, Abe ran his finger through the ejaculate and then popped it into his mouth. "Mmm," he moaned. "Love that taste."

Jason groaned. "I want to see you do that again." He gripped Abe's hair and pulled his head back until their eyes met. "Tell me you'll let me cum in your mouth if I get tested." He tugged. "Tell me I can coat your damn tongue with it and watch your face when you swallow."

Abe went from interested to hard all over again. "I'd let you." He licked his lips. "I'd love it."

"Christ." Jason dropped his head against the back of the couch. "I'll go tomorrow." He dipped two fingers into the liquid on Abe's belly and then painted Abe's lip with it. "Going to feed you from my cock, baby."

Whimpering, Abe parted his lips and took Jason's fingers into his mouth. He fellated them like they were Jason's dick, moaning and humping against Jason's stomach.

"You keep that up and you're going to get fucked right now," Jason said as he pumped his fingers in and out of Abe's mouth and plucked Abe's nipples with his free hand.

Abe moaned and sucked harder.

"Damn, look at you. So sexy." Jason pulled his fingers away, cupped his hand around the back of Abe's head, and yanked him forward for a bruising kiss. "I have condoms in my wallet but no lube, and I'm not doing you dry, so we need to go to the bedroom." He nipped Abe's lower lip and tugged it between his teeth before releasing him. "Unless you keep some out here." He flicked his gaze around the room and frowned. "Who decorated this place?"

"My roommate," Abe answered, his words sounding slurred to his own ears. Every part of his body was heavy with satisfaction.

"You have a roommate?" Jason asked in surprise.

"Uh-huh. It's her apartment, actually. I sublet her spare room."

"How is it I didn't know you had a roommate?"

"It hasn't come up," Abe said with shrug. "She stays at her boyfriend's place, so she's never around. I haven't seen her in weeks."

"Weeks? I've been coming over for *months* and I've never seen any indication of a roommate."

Grinning, Abe said, "You've only been here four times, and based on your expression when you noticed the flower patterns on the furniture and the cat figurines, I gather you weren't paying close attention to the decor."

"It was always dark," Jason said defensively. "Besides—" He bit Abe's chin and fondled his package. "I paid attention where it mattered."

No argument there. "True enough," Abe said. "Anyway, I have a roommate. Her name is Cindy. She's a teacher too, but elementary school. And this is her apartment."

"But she's never here?"

"Right."

"Because she's with her boyfriend."

"Uh-huh."

"So why doesn't she just move in with him instead of wasting money on rent?"

"Because they're not married and Cindy's, like, really super religious."

"Religious?" Jason arched his eyebrows.

Abe nodded.

"And her religion says if you're shacking up with your boyfriend and probably screwing each other silly, you have to keep your own apartment on the side?"

"I have no idea," Abe said with a laugh. "All I know is she wants a ring and she doesn't have one yet, so I get a great deal on rent because I pay for a bedroom and get a furnished apartment."

"I'm not sure the furnished part is all that great a deal," Jason said as he looked around again.

"It's fine." Abe shrugged. "I make $33,000 a year. This place is way better than anything else I could afford on my own."

"You spend all day with teenagers and that's all they pay you?" Jason asked incredulously. "Are you kidding me?"

"I'm a high school teacher," Abe reminded him. "Not a doctor." He paused. "By the way, Dr. Garcia, I don't think you ever told me exactly what you do."

"Surgery. Cardiothoracic surgery."

"Wow." Abe wasn't surprised. Jason was smart and aggressive, so it was easy to imagine him as a surgeon. "I'm impressed." He pressed his lips together to hold in his smile and tried to sound serious when he said, "That means you make way more than $33,000 a year, right?"

Jason scoffed and rolled his eyes.

"Cool." Abe climbed off Jason's lap and waggled his eyebrows playfully. "I'm dating a rich guy. You can buy me stuff," he joked.

"Dating?"

His heart stopping, Abe looked at Jason and swallowed hard. "Aren't we?" He licked his lips. "Dating, I mean?"

Jason stood and pulled up his pants. "Not so far, no." He looked into Abe's eyes and brushed a wayward lock of hair off his forehead. "What are you doing tomorrow night?"

"I don't know. Nothing right now."

Jason leaned down and bussed his lips over Abe's cheek. "Good. I'm taking you out to a fancy dinner."

"You are?" Abe asked in surprise.

"Yeah. If I'm supposed to be some kind of sugar daddy, I've really got to up my game. I'm pretty sure I haven't spent a dime on you so far."

"Excellent point." Abe let Jason take his hand and lead him to the bedroom. "What do you say you splurge and treat us to a movie too?"

"Dinner and a movie?" Jason said, his expression wistful.

"With popcorn," Abe added.

Jason nodded. "With popcorn."

"And Milk Duds mixed in it."

"Milk Duds mixed with the popcorn?"

"Yup." Abe nodded. "They get all melty. It's good."

"Got it. Dinner. Movie. Popcorn. Milk Duds." Jason smiled softly. "It's a date."

Chapter 7

JASON WOKE up on Saturday morning to the feeling of Abe's warm body cuddled in his arms. His chest was pressed to Abe's back, his arm was snaked around Abe's waist, and his thigh was pressed between Abe's knees. He tightened his hold and shifted closer, smiling when his erection settled easily in the cleft of Abe's ass.

Though he made a muffled sound, Abe didn't wake up. Jason decided he could take care of that problem. He rocked his hips back and forth as he gnawed his way across Abe's neck and shoulders and caressed Abe's chest.

"I'm trying to sleep," Abe mumbled.

"I'm trying to wake you up." Jason swirled his tongue around Abe's earlobe and then suckled it.

"I'm sleeping."

"I'm horny."

Abe pushed his ass against Jason, moaned, and said, "Do you have another condom?"

"Mmm-hmm," Jason said as he gripped Abe's hip and began rocking them together.

"'Kay. Get it and fuck me. Then we're going back to sleep."

"Look at you making demands. Aren't you supposed to be the sweet, restrained one?" Jason said with a chuckle.

"Uh-huh. I was a good boy before I met you and you turned me into a trollop. Go get the rubber. I'm horny too."

"I like that about you," Jason said.

"That I'm horny?"

Jason licked a swath up Abe's neck. "That you're sweet and good and restrained and horny as fuck." He dropped his palm to Abe's balls and fondled them.

"It's your fault."

Smiling, Jason kissed Abe's neck and then began sucking on it while he squeezed his nuts.

"You're going to leave a mark."

Jason's cock got harder at that idea.

"What if I do it below your shirt line?" He had no idea why he was pressing the issue, or even suggesting it to begin with. He wasn't into hickeys or marks.

"'Kay," Abe said, his voice husky. "Then nobody else will see it."

Groaning, Jason scooted down and bit Abe's back. *Nobody else.* He licked his way to Abe's side and began sucking. *Only me.* Not being the possessive type, he wasn't sure why the idea of Abe not being with anyone else turned him on, but the wetness forming at the tip of his cock and his tightly drawn balls wouldn't let him deny it.

"Slick yourself up," he said, his voice rough with arousal. He pushed himself up and bit Abe's ass. "I need to fuck you now." He slid off the bed, found his pants, and got another condom out of his wallet—he'd need to restock when he got home or buy a box for Abe's apartment. He fumbled with the condom, eventually getting the packet open and the damn thing rolled on. "Are you rea—" Jason turned back around and groaned at the sight that greeted him. Abe was lying on his back, his legs spread and raised, two fingers up his own ass. "Fuck, that's hot." Jason leaped onto the bed, pulled Abe's hand away, and with no hesitation plunged into tight heat. "Yes," he hissed.

"Jase!" Abe arched underneath him, exposing his pale neck.

"Feel good, baby?" he asked as he leaned over Abe's lithe body. "You like being filled up?"

His blue eyes wide and full of passion, Abe stared at him.

Jason slowly slid out while he skated his palms over Abe's arms and hoarsely said, "You do, don't you?" He gripped Abe's hands in his, held him down, and said, "You love being fucked," while he shoved in hard, stretching the tiny hole to capacity.

Abe wailed underneath him, wrapping his legs around Jason's hips and bucking.

"Yeah, you do." Jason pulled out and then pushed back in again. "You fucking love it." He bit Abe's chin. "Does anybody know that about you?" he asked while he continued the steady in-and-out motion, pummeling Abe's body. "Does anybody else know what a dirty boy you are?"

Abe's nostrils flared as he dragged in big gusts of air.

"I bet they don't." Jason pressed all the way inside and circled his hips, grinding into Abe. "I bet they see those big blue eyes and that pretty blond hair and think you're an untouchable angel." He slowly pulled out. "But you're not, are you?" He licked Abe's lips. "Not deep down."

His gaze locked with Jason's, Abe slowly shook his head.

"I know, baby," Jason said. He grinned evilly. "Don't worry, I know, and I'll give you what you need." He pulled out of Abe's ass, groaning at the loss, and then flipped him over and rammed back in.

"Ah!" Abe shouted.

Pressing his hands on Abe's upper back, Jason held him captive against the bed. He steadied himself on his knees and slammed inside as hard as he could.

His moans muffled by the mattress, Abe squirmed underneath him and blindly reached back. He finally made contact with Jason's leg and hung on as though he needed the connection.

"I'm here," Jason grunted as he thrust in and out of Abe. He had never fucked anyone with so much force and aggression. "I'm here and I'll take care of you."

He lowered himself on top of Abe, blanketing his slim body with his own wide frame, and bit whatever parts of Abe's back and shoulders he could reach while continuing his harsh plunges.

"I'm going to fill you up," Jason said a couple of minutes later. "Going to make you shoot so hard."

He grabbed Abe's hips, yanked his pelvis up, and reached underneath his body for his dick. It only took a squeeze and a rough yank and Abe was creaming over his hand and shouting into the mattress. Hot ejaculate was still streaming over Jason's fingers when his own orgasm hit. He opened his mouth in a soundless wail and stilled as his balls emptied deep inside Abe's welcoming body.

Time disappeared in the wake of intense pleasure, but eventually Jason regained his breath and enough brain capacity to slide out of Abe and get rid of the full condom. He tied it off and dropped it on the floor, promising himself he'd clean up when his legs worked again, and then he planted his palms on the bed and pushed himself up so Abe could move.

"Turn over," he said.

Abe whimpered but didn't change positions.

"Turn over, baby." Jason kissed his shoulder, held on to his waist, and flipped him onto his back. "I want to see your gorgeous face."

Abe's eyes were closed, his cheeks were wet with tears, and his chest heaved as he gasped for air. Jason liked to think he was decent in bed, sometimes even good, but he had never made a guy cry with ecstasy. Then again, he had never before spent as much time with a guy, never kissed and fondled and caressed anyone, never focused on anything other than getting off fast. Not until he met Abe.

"Shh." Jason peppered kisses over Abe's face and licked up the salty wetness. "You're okay." He put his palm on Abe's chest. "Slow and steady."

Eventually, Abe's breathing slowed and he opened his eyes and gazed at Jason. The worshipful expression on his face would stay with Jason forever. He had saved people's lives and they had never looked at him with such reverence. Tenderness wove through him and settled in his chest, making him ache.

"There you are," he said, smiling at Abe.

Abe reached up and ran his fingertips down the side of Jason's face.

Jason grasped his wrist and held his hand in place as he turned into it and kissed his palm. "Let's clean up and then we can go back to sleep for a little while."

"Okay," Abe said, his voice soft. "Can you...." He swallowed hard. "Do you have time to stay for breakfast later?"

"Yes." Jason nodded. "I'll need to go home and take care of some things before our date tonight, but I have time for a nap and breakfast. I'll even help cook."

"That sounds perfect." Abe smiled and sighed contentedly. "Really perfect."

Sex first thing in the morning, sleeping with Abe in his arms, making breakfast together, and a dinner date in the evening, followed by more sex. It sounded pretty perfect to Jason too.

"HOW MUCH have I missed?" Jason asked as he sat down on the grass next to Angela's camping chair and squinted at the kids running across the field.

"They just started the second half," she said. "So you're here earlier than usual."

"I wasn't working today."

"Donny's games are on weekends. You don't usually work on weekends."

Ignoring the comment, Jason said, "How's he playing?"

"Fine. He hasn't scored but he had a few nice assists. He'll be happy you're here."

"That'd be new." His son wasn't the happy type. The boy was surly and disrespectful. Angela was way too easy on him.

"You can't expect a smile or anything obvious. But if we're really lucky, he'll come over and grunt at us. That's how you'll know he's happy."

"If *he's* really lucky, I'll grunt back," Jason grumbled.

Angela turned her head to the side, lowered her sunglasses, and stared at Jason over the top of them. "Donny is thirteen. What's your excuse?"

"I'm thirty-six."

Shaking her head, she pushed her sunglasses back up and said, "At least we know where he gets it."

Jason grunted.

"So," Angela said.

He waited for her to continue her sentence, but she didn't. He had nothing else to do, so he said, "Yeah?"

"What are you up to next Saturday?"

Angela never asked about his social life. Never. He frowned and looked at her. "Why do you want to know?"

"No reason," she said too lightly. It wasn't sincere. "Just making small talk." She didn't make small talk. It was a setup of some sort. For what, he didn't know.

He turned back to the game and kept his mouth shut. It was safer.

"It's Valentine's Day," she said, apropos of nothing.

"Uh-huh," Jason replied, because it was.

"The good restaurants get booked up. If you don't have a reservation, it's impossible to get in."

For the first time in his life, Jason had planned a Valentine's evening, so he was aware of the reservation rule. He also knew flower orders had to be placed well in advance. Thankfully, he had done both, and in a weird twist, he'd enjoyed it. He was looking forward to taking Abe out and romancing him. Not that he'd ever admit that to anyone, himself included.

It had been a month since he and Abe had decided to date, but they'd only been out a few times. Jason had his kids every other weekend. Weekdays were hard because of work. And the first few hours they saw each other, they were both so hot for it they couldn't go out in public. Plus, Abe was as much of a homebody as Jason, who only ever went out to get laid. But even though it was a made-up holiday, Jason figured they'd both enjoy doing something special on Valentine's Day.

"So do you have reservations?"

Jason snapped his gaze toward Angela. "What are you rambling on about?"

"Dinner reservations for Saturday. Do you have them?"

"Why are you asking me about dinner reservations?"

"Because, like I said, it's Valentine's Day, so I assume you'll be going out to dinner with your boyfriend and I want to make sure you know to make reservations. Otherwise you'll show up somewhere, get turned away, and get angry." She shook her head. "There is nothing romantic about you throwing a tantrum."

"I have no idea what you're rattling on and on about."

"Valentine's Day."

She was baiting him. That had to be it. There was no way she knew what he had planned. Even if she had an inkling he was seeing someone, which she didn't, she wouldn't expect him to organize a special night out. He wasn't that kind of person. Of course, he did in fact have such a night planned, but that was neither here nor there.

"I'm done with this conversation," he said.

"Don't be an ass. I'm trying to help you."

"Did I ask you for help?"

"No. But I'm giving it to you anyway because that's just the kind of person I am."

"There are at least ten insults I can come up with in response to that comment, but I'm keeping them to myself because you're the mother of my children."

"Ten?" Angela snorted. "Jason, honey, I've amassed way more than that many insults for you over the years."

And each one of them was probably well-earned. "Touché," he said.

She reached over her shoulder and patted herself on the back.

"I wasn't trying to be an asshole," Jason said.

"It's okay. I know you can't help it."

"Screw off."

"That remorse didn't last long."

"Whatever."

"Very grown-up response," Angela said. "Anyway, back to our discussion."

"We weren't having a discussion." It was an inquisition.

"Do you have reservations for Valentine's Day?"

"If I had any energy at all, I'd get up and sit somewhere else."

"No, you wouldn't. You like me way too much."

He adored her. "Doesn't mean I want to hear you talk."

"Answer my question and I'll stop."

"Oh, please. Do you think I'm new?" Jason said. "If I answer one question, you'll just continue down your list to the next one. I'm pretty much fucked until the last whistle blows."

"In that case, you may as well humor me."

"How about we skip over whatever groundwork you're laying here and get to the point of this interrogation?" Jason said.

"Are you seeing Kristen's old math teacher?"

Immediately, Jason regretted having pushed Angela. He probably could have successfully given her the runaround for the rest of the game and gotten away relatively unscathed. Now he was stuck and on the verge of panic.

"Calm down, Jason. We're not married anymore. You're allowed to see people." She pushed her sunglasses onto her head and looked him in the eyes. "You're allowed to see *men*."

He knew that. Of course he knew that. But casually talking about it was difficult because he had spent most of his life denying it and hiding it, and being ashamed of not being able to deny it and being bad at hiding it.

"I don't know how to talk about this with you," he admitted.

"Hey. We're friends, right? Isn't that what we always say?" Angela reached down for his hand. "Besides, I stopped being mad a long time ago."

He put his palm in hers and squeezed it. "I'm sorry."

"I know," she said. "We both made mistakes, but that's in the past."

"No." He shook his head, unwilling to let Angela shoulder the blame for his shortcomings. "It was my fault. I'm the one who cheated. I'm the one who couldn't…. It was my fault."

"You shouldn't have cheated," she conceded. "But I made mistakes too, and I shouldn't have married you when we barely knew each other."

"We knew each other enough. Besides, you were pregnant."

Angela turned her face to the game but didn't seem to be watching the action on the field. "Being pregnant isn't a reason to get married."

"Of course it is!" Jason said. "It's the best reason. Marriage is for family."

Sighing, Angela looked at him again. "Having a family is a great part of it," she said. "But it's not the reason to commit your life to someone. It just isn't. Kids grow up and move out, and then what?"

"I don't know," Jason said, frustrated.

"That's because you think about food more than you think about the future."

"That's not true," Jason said.

"No?" she said.

"No." Jason smiled and tried to lighten the mood. "I think about sex more than I think about the future."

Tossing her long brown hair over her shoulder, Angela laughed. "That is *so* true."

After giving her hand one last squeeze, Jason let go and rested his forearms on his knees. "I'm glad we can be like this."

"I am too, but I think it's time both of us figure out what we want out of life."

"What do you mean?"

"We got married when we were twenty-one, had Kristen when we were twenty-two, Donald when we were twenty-four, and squeezed in medical school and residencies along the way. I've barely had time to breathe, let alone think about myself."

"I had time to figure out I'm gay."

"I'm pretty sure you knew that going in."

"I don't know." Jason shrugged. "Maybe I did. Doesn't matter now."

"No, it doesn't. And it's not what I meant, anyway. I'm talking about figuring out what we want out of life. For as long as I can remember, it was all about school and grades and being well-rounded so I could get into a good college and then medical school, and now I'm done with all that. I got in. I graduated. I have a good job. I met all my goals." She sighed. "Now what?"

"I always wanted a family," Jason said quietly. "That was my goal."

"You have one," Angela said.

"I know, but…." He shook his head. "Never mind."

"It's not the way you thought it'd be?"

He shrugged.

"It'll never be like the picture you had in your head growing up, Jason. But you know what? You have two amazing kids and a fantastic ex-wife."

Jason chuckled and nodded. "That I do."

"And I think if you decide you want to, you can have someone to share it with."

"Maybe," he conceded. The conversation reminded him of the one he'd had with his cousin Asher a couple of months earlier. But this time around, it made more sense, either because it was Angela talking or because he'd had Abe as a steady presence in his life and he now knew firsthand there was more to being with a guy than sex. But there was a long distance between a steady presence and what his parents shared. He looked out at the field.

"So?" Angela asked.

Shaking his head, Jason smiled and said, "Yes, I made reservations for Valentine's Day."

"And?"

He sighed resignedly. "And I'm dating Kristen's former math teacher. I have no idea how you figured that out."

"From the way you looked at him during the meeting and the fact you knew his first name when nobody had said it." She tapped her head. "I'm not just a pretty face."

"I know. You're gorgeous."

"I've had two kids."

"And you're still the most beautiful woman I've ever met."

She patted his shoulder and stretched her legs forward. "You have to say that. You love me."

"I do. No matter what I did, I hope you know I always loved you. I just—"

"I know. I've always loved you the same way. But I think I'm ready for a different kind of love." She glanced at him. "How about you?"

"I haven't thought about it."

They sat quietly and watched their son run across the field. He was good, better than Jason remembered. Of course, he usually got to the soccer games so late he only saw Donny play for a few minutes.

"I think I should spend more time with the kids."

"They're your kids. We have shared custody. Nobody's stopping you."

"I'm not sure I'm ready for them to know I'm seeing someone," he admitted. "Don't tell them."

"Oh, Jason," she said sadly. "You're not doing anything wrong."

He shrugged. "They're my kids."

"Yes. They're your kids. They love you. And they know you're gay."

They knew because Angela had insisted on telling them, saying she wouldn't allow deceit in their family. *Their* family. Even after he broke it apart. He was too thankful for the sentiment to be angry.

"Knowing and seeing aren't the same, so don't tell them about Abe, okay?"

"They won't care that you're dating someone or that the someone is a man."

"I'll think about it."

"Kristen already adores him," Angela pointed out.

The whistle blew and the kids started running toward the sidelines.

"Saved by the bell," Jason said.

"We're not done with this conversation."

Of that he had no doubt. He might even be grateful.

Chapter **8**

"HI, JASE," Abe said as he answered his phone. "How was work?"

"It was work." Jason sighed, and Abe could imagine him rubbing his palm over his eye. "Anyway, I'm done now and I'm on my way over."

"About that." Abe cleared his throat and lowered his voice. Though his bedroom door was closed, the apartment walls were pretty thin. "Cindy's here."

"Cindy?"

"My roommate."

"Oh." There was a pause. "Why is she there?"

"Well, technically it's her apartment, and she had a fight with her boyfriend. She wants a ring and he hasn't stepped up, so she moved back in."

"I don't blame her," Jason said. "What's he waiting for? She's been essentially living with the guy since before I met you and that was, what? Almost seven months ago. They've been together plenty long enough for him to get to know her. She's not getting any younger, and if she wants a family, she can't waste her time with someone who isn't serious about her."

When Abe first met Jason in September, all he'd hoped for was one night of fun. A couple of months later when he saw him again, he knew the sex would be good and anything else nonexistent. More than two months passed before he saw Jason again, but by the time they went to bed the third time, Abe was confident both of them wanted to get to know each other better. That was in early January, and as they neared the end of March, he felt more emotionally connected to Jason than he ever had to anyone else.

With Jason, he could be a simple guy from Utah who taught school and liked sitting at home reading books or playing Sudoku puzzles instead of going out to bars and never once be called boring. He could crack up at commercials of animals wearing clothes or driving cars and glance up to see Jason looking at him like he was something special instead of rolling his eyes at his sense of humor. And he could spend an evening on his knees worshiping Jason's cock, or on his back with his legs in the air begging to be fucked, get coated in cum, and then meet a gaze that was adoring with not an ounce of derision. With Jason, Abe flourished, including the parts of himself he usually kept locked down and hidden away, and for the first time in his life, he felt whole.

The idea of losing that, of losing Jason, was like a hard kick to the gut, making Abe's stomach roll and his lungs seize. And yet Abe knew better than to push Jason about what he saw in their future or even how he defined their present. Because despite being with Abe seemingly every moment he wasn't working or with his kids, despite sharing stories about his childhood and anecdotes about his job, despite spending hours taking Abe to the heights of pleasure, and despite wrapping himself around Abe at night and holding him close until morning, Jason hadn't introduced Abe to anyone in his life, hadn't invited Abe to his home, and hadn't spoken of a future with Abe in it.

Did that mean Jason was no different than Cindy's boyfriend? Did it mean he wasn't, in Jason's own words, serious about Abe? And would it matter if it did, or could Abe be satisfied rolling along as they were, with Jason at the center of his life in some ways and a stranger in others?

"I'm beat but I guess instead of making dinner, we can grab a bite at a sports bar while we watch the game." Jason sighed. "Just tell me Cindy goes to bed early and she's a really heavy sleeper, because I haven't seen you since Tuesday, and three days is about as long as I can go without fucking you before I start losing it and snapping at innocent bystanders."

Abe chuckled, partially because the comment was funny and partially because it was true. He didn't know anyone with as high a sex drive as Jason's.

"I'm not sure why you're laughing," Jason said. "I bet you're crawling up the walls right now too."

Correction. He didn't know anyone other than himself with as high a sex drive as Jason's.

"I'm better than you at dealing with dry spells," Abe said.

"Uh-huh, right," Jason said disbelievingly.

"I am!"

"You sure about that?" Jason asked, the tenor of his voice dropping dangerously.

Though he knew he should be wary of whatever Jason had planned, Abe was too invested in his position to back away. Plus, he was curious about what Jason would do to prove his point. So he said, "Yes."

"Did I tell you what I've been thinking about when I've jacked off in the shower these last few days?"

Abe's breath hitched at the immediate visual that slammed into his head: Jason naked, wet, and hard. "No," he said.

"I was thinking about how much you love my cock."

Denying the statement or calling Jason arrogant was futile because he was right. The long, thick shaft, darker than Jason's deeply tan skin, made Abe's mouth water.

"Last time I saw you, I couldn't get you away from it."

After work on Tuesday, Jason had come to Abe's apartment. They'd made dinner, eaten at the small kitchen table, and chatted about nothing in particular before going to bed, where Abe settled between Jason's thighs and traced every vein on his magnificent dick with his tongue.

"I don't remember you complaining," Abe said huskily, his mouth watering and his own dick swelling at the memory.

"It's not a complaint, baby. I love the noises you make when you're going down on me."

"Noises?" Abe asked hoarsely.

"Mmm-hmm. They're these quiet little moans, almost like whimpers. Turns me on to hear how into it you get."

Breathing heavily, Abe leaned against the wall and dropped his hand down the front of his jeans.

"I bet you're touching yourself right now, just from thinking about it," Jason said. "You want to know the part that gets me the hottest?"

"Uh-huh."

"When I came and you opened your mouth and took it all in on your tongue. I fucking love how eager you were to taste it, and when I was done, do you remember what you did?"

Abe whimpered.

"That's right. You rubbed my cock all over your face, didn't you? Those pretty lips and round cheeks, your eyelids and neck, you got 'em all slick while you jerked yourself off."

"Jase," Abe said breathlessly.

"Uh-huh."

"I don't want to go out." Abe licked his lips. "I want us to get naked so I can suck your cock and ride you while you're watching the game."

"Come over to my place," Jason growled. "I'll order pizza."

"Your three favorite things all at the same time," Abe said with a strained laugh. His balls ached.

"Hanging out with you, fucking you, and eating dinner with you?" Jason asked in confusion.

"College basketball, pizza, and fucking," Abe reminded him.

"Oh. Right." Jason paused. "I may have to amend my list."

And just like that, Abe got the answers to his questions—no, he wouldn't be happy living on the sidelines of Jason's life indefinitely, and yes, Jason was serious about him, but he didn't quite know it yet or maybe he didn't know what to do about it. Thankfully, Abe had a lot of patience and plenty of time to figure out how to get both of them where they wanted to be.

"HI." ABE leaned up for a kiss as he walked into Jason's house.

"Hi, baby." Jason pushed the door closed, cupped both sides of Abe's face, dipped down, and covered Abe's lips. He lingered, licking and nibbling, tugging Abe's lower lip between his own before slipping his tongue in and then beginning the process over again. "Mmm," he sighed when he pulled away. "I missed that."

Dazed, Abe blinked up at him. "You're a great kisser."

"It's easy when I enjoy it so much." He smiled, and Abe's heart throbbed. However long it took for them to move forward with their relationship, he would wait. He wasn't in a rush, and his dream of a white-picket-fence life with a forever guy had morphed into a longing for a forever life with *this* guy.

"What's in the bags?" Jason asked, reaching for Abe's hands.

"Groceries." Abe handed half the bags over. "I'd already gone shopping before Cindy came home, so I brought everything here. Now we're set for the weekend." He held his breath and braced himself for Jason's reaction. They had discussed an evening watching the college basketball tournament, not a weekend holed up together in Jason's townhouse.

Looking from the bags to Abe, Jason furrowed his brow, his shoulders tense and his lips stretched into thin lines.

"Jase, if I overstepped, I'm sorry," Abe said, trying to sound nonchalant despite his disappointment. He had never felt as safe and calm as he did going to bed with Jason's bulk wrapped around him, and he didn't want that aspect of their weekend plans to change. *Patience*, he reminded himself. "I can put most of this back in the car right now and store the chicken, eggs, milk, and cheese in your fridge until I leave tonight."

"You're not leaving tonight." Jason turned on his heel and walked into the townhouse.

Not sure what else to do, Abe followed.

"I barely got to see you this week, and I've been looking forward to spending the weekend with you," Jason said. They reached the kitchen, and Jason dropped the bags on the counter. The jars inside rattled from the force of impact. "There's no difference between being together here and being together at your apartment." He yanked the refrigerator door open. "Even if your roommate wasn't there, it'd make more sense for us to stay here because your TV is practically an antique and I have a sixty-five-inch LED." He grabbed one of the bags and put it into his nearly empty refrigerator. "Plus, your bed is a queen-size and mine's a king, so my legs don't hang over the edge."

Assuming Jason was talking to himself, Abe remained silent and waited for him to work through whatever was bothering him.

"The housekeeper comes on Thursdays, so my sheets are clean." Jason picked up the other bag he had set down and wedged it next to the first one. "I have plenty of pillows."

Curling his lips over his teeth, Abe tried not to laugh.

"Are there any more bags?" Jason asked as he darted his gaze around the room.

"Just these." Abe held up his hands.

"I'll take them," Jason said, reaching out for the bags.

"Jase?" Abe said softly.

"Yeah?"

"Do you think the fridge is the best place for spaghetti, pasta sauce, canned artichokes, bananas, pita chips...." Abe took a breath. "Should I keep going with the grocery list?"

"No." Jason shook his head. "I think you made your point." He gave Abe a tight, forced smile. "Show me what you got for us, and we can put everything away in the right places." He turned back to the refrigerator, took out the two bags he'd put in, and set them on the counter.

"Do you want to talk about it?" Abe asked quietly as he walked over to Jason and put his own bags down.

He expected Jason to brush off the question or pretend he had no idea what Abe meant, and at first, it seemed that was exactly what he planned to do, because he squared his shoulders, pursed his lips, and glanced away.

Staying quiet, Abe stood next to Jason, leaned against him, tipped his head to the side, and rested it against Jason's shoulder.

After a few seconds, Jason softened his posture. "I've never brought a man into my home," he said as he rubbed his palms over his eyes. "Not before I got married." He turned around and rested his back against the counter. "Not in the five years since my divorce." He looked across the room instead of at Abe and quietly said, "Not when I was married."

"Why?"

Jason shrugged, turned back to the counter, and started emptying the bags.

One end of Jason's kitchen curved in a peninsula. Three stools were tucked underneath it. Wanting to give Jason space, Abe walked over, pulled a stool out, and sat down.

Jason was halfway done emptying the second bag when he spoke. "Home is for family."

There was a world of meaning behind the deceptively simple comment, but having a conversation about it was like navigating a minefield. Rather than walking into a war zone, Abe decided to cheer Jason up the old-fashioned way. He kicked off his flip-flops, stood up, and pushed his jeans and briefs to the floor.

Apparently having heard the clothes hit the ground, Jason turned around. "What are you doing?" he asked.

Abe stepped to the side and moved past the counter and cabinets blocking Jason's view of his lower half. "You seem, uh, down. I thought this might cheer you up."

After snapping his gaze to Abe's groin, Jason looked back up and smiled affectionately. "You're not all that up yourself," he pointed out, his tone amused.

"Take off your pants and I'll get there."

Cupping himself through his pants, Jason arched his eyebrows. "Just the sight of my cock turns you on?"

His gaze glued to Jason's large hand fondling his package, Abe's dick swelled and rose. "You know it does."

"I do know and I like it." Jason crooked his finger and said, "C'mere."

Seeing Jason happy wiped away most of Abe's tension. He walked over, his focus on Jason's face. As soon as he was within reach, Jason shot his hand out, snaked his arm around Abe's back, and yanked him forward.

"I'm sorry." Jason hunched down and cupped both of Abe's bare buttcheeks, squeezing and massaging. "You shouldn't have to seduce me to get me to act like a decent person."

"I don't know anything about seducing." Abe shrugged. "But having sex with you is never a hardship."

"Oh, I can't agree with that," Jason said, his voice low and deep. He rocked his hips, rubbing up against Abe's exposed erection. "I'd say it got plenty hard."

"You're on a roll with the bad jokes," Abe said with a laugh.

Dipping down, Jason brushed his lips over Abe's. "I wanted to hear you laugh."

Abe sighed, relieved the tense atmosphere was gone, replaced by their usual comfort and ease with each other. He laid his cheek against Jason's chest and wound his arms around Jason's waist. Jason kissed the top of his head and rubbed circles on his back.

"Angela and I met our junior year at an MCAT study class. We'd only been dating for about three months when we found out she was pregnant. That part was harder on her than it was on me."

"I'd say so, yeah," Abe said teasingly.

"Behave." Jason pinched his ass. "I'm unburdening my soul here."

"Sorry." Abe kissed the base of Jason's throat. "I'm listening."

"I grew up with a lot of family around. My sisters you know about."

"One's in California and the other is in Chicago, right?"

"Uh-huh. Plus I have a million cousins, and as kids we were always going back and forth to people's houses, running around. That was family in my head, and I expected to have the same thing. Angela is really wonderful and when she told me the news, I was so happy. I got down on one knee right there and proposed. She was crying and scared. Having a kid and getting married wasn't in her life plan right then. She wanted to be a doctor. But she said yes and she ended up being a great mom, really great. She's an incredible doctor, too, and she was a good wife."

"She sounds amazing," Abe said quietly.

"You'd love her," Jason said. "Everyone loves her." His lips turned up at the sides, but his eyes were sad. "I love her."

"Just not the way a husband is supposed to?" Abe said in understanding.

"No." Jason shook his head. "Not that way. She knew pretty early on."

"That you're gay?" Abe asked.

"Yes. I didn't realize it, but she told me later that she figured it out. Angela is damn smart. Nothing gets past her. But we were good friends, still are, so she said she hoped it would be enough. I think I was hoping I'd change, that somehow everything would click into place the way it was supposed to. But it never did, and I got frustrated and mad and—" Jason swallowed hard. "I cheated on her. She knew. She didn't say anything, but she knew."

"Why didn't she confront you?"

Raising his face so he was looking at the ceiling, Jason said, "She was pregnant the first time." He shook his head. "God, I'm such an asshole." He sighed. "She was pregnant with Kristen. We were newly married, both of us starting medical school. Life was different then— busier, harder. I think she didn't have time to deal with it. I don't know. I never asked her why she let it go, but looking back on it now, I'm sure she knew what I was doing even back then. Eventually, she confronted me. I promised I wouldn't do it again, and we ended up with another surprise pregnancy—Donny is thirteen." Jason cleared his throat. "Anyway, long story short, I did it again, she found out, I pleaded for one more chance, and she gave it to me. I didn't stop, and when we finished our residencies and finally started living a normal life, she said both of us deserved better and that our kids deserved to be raised with models of a healthy relationship. She filed for divorce. I begged her not to go through with it, swore up and down I'd change, but like I said, Angela is damn smart so"—he shrugged—"we're divorced."

Abe wasn't surprised by Jason's story. He knew enough people with young families to be familiar with their busy schedules and hurried lives. And it didn't take much of a stretch to imagine Jason having a wandering eye and acting on it.

"Say something," Jason said, and Abe realized he was looking at him worriedly.

"What?"

"I remember how upset you were when you thought I was married. I know you have an opinion about what I just told you."

"An opinion?"

"Not an opinion, but—" Jason sucked in air. "Are you disgusted by me?"

"I don't like what you did and I think we need to talk about some things, but no, I'm not disgusted by *you*."

"What things?"

Abe's mind was a jumble of thoughts about Jason's past and their future. "I need to sort it out."

Jason tugged him closer, holding on tightly.

"We're okay," Abe promised as he caressed the side of Jason's neck. Regardless of what he didn't know, he was certain he wanted Jason in his life. He wouldn't let past mistakes take away the future they could build together. "Let's get the groceries sorted out, order that pizza, and watch the game."

With a nod, Jason stepped back and started gathering items for the fridge. "Where're you going?" he asked when Abe walked to where he'd taken off his clothes.

"To get my pants."

"No."

Abe turned around. "No?"

"Nuh-uh." Jason shook his head. "I think the shirt-on-pants-off look is sexy on you. I suffered through a trip down memory lane and a painful conversation, the least you can do is keep the goods exposed."

Looking down, Abe saw his dick hanging below the bottom hem of his shirt. He shrugged and returned to the counter. If Jason got off on seeing him partially dressed, he'd stay partially dressed. In fact, he was hard-pressed to think of something he wouldn't do to turn Jason on. Which was why when Abe returned to the counter, he reached for the farthest bag, twisting so his backside faced Jason and stretching as far as he could.

"Plus," Jason said huskily as he grazed his big hand over Abe's fully exposed ass and wiggled his fingertips into Abe's channel, "this way I can play with you during the game."

Yup, Abe was all for turning Jason on.

Chapter 9

HAVING THE man he was sleeping with in the same space his children occupied when they stayed with him was a merging of two parts of Jason's life that he had always meticulously kept separate. As a result, he was on edge and Abe's first visit to his townhouse had started out awkwardly. But the initial tension had melted away quickly and they'd had a great weekend watching basketball, cooking side by side in Jason's spacious kitchen, and burning up the sheets.

The first time Abe had cuddled against him on his deep, suede sofa and looked at his flat-screen TV, he had turned to Jason and said they should rent movies instead of going out. A blow job/hand job combination followed shortly after, driving the point home for Jason. When he stopped thinking and lived in the moment, he loved having Abe in his space. So much so that the one Friday night, which had turned into a weekend, had ended up lasting more than a week.

Abe was off work for spring break and Jason had a light schedule, so Monday, when Jason was working, Abe went home, threw some clothes in a bag, and came back using the spare key. He spent some time catching up on his grading, but the rest of the week he helped Jason with projects he'd been putting off around the house—organizing his office, fixing the leaky sink in the hallway bathroom, replacing burned-out lightbulbs in various rooms, cleaning out his closet. Some things they did together, others Abe handled when Jason was at work, and all of it felt so natural that Jason didn't consciously realize they had spent nine nights in a row together until he crawled into his empty bed on Sunday and was hit with a pang of loneliness.

Angela had taken the kids to visit her parents in Florida over spring break. She had an intense schedule at work waiting for her when she returned. Jason wanted to spend more time with his children, so he said he'd take them for the next week, which meant Abe had to go back to his apartment.

Being a single father for a week straight was harder than Jason had expected. Kristen, at fifteen, was self-sufficient. She kept her things contained in her bedroom, did her homework without prompting, and was ready to leave for school on time every day. But Jason still had to drive her places, make sure he had food she could pack for lunch, cook dinner, and help with any number of little issues that came up.

Donny, his thirteen-year-old, didn't ask for help with anything, but he seemed to make a conscious effort to create problems. He left his things everywhere—shoes in front of the door, jacket on the kitchen floor, backpack in the middle of the hallway. He didn't clean up after himself, so Jason regularly walked into the kitchen to find crumbs and a knife, sticky with jelly or another substance on his previously pristine granite countertop, or a carton of milk left out so long it wasn't cold to the touch and had to be tossed. Towels littered the bathroom floor after Donny showered, toothpaste was sprayed on the mirror when he bothered to brush his teeth, and the boy either had the worst aim known to man, or he was intentionally pissing on the floor instead of in the toilet bowl. And when Donny spoke to anyone, which was rare, it was to make a snide remark. After the first day, Jason stopped telling him to get off his phone and decided to be grateful for anything that kept Donny occupied and out of his way.

The week after his kids went back to their mother's house, Jason had no time to recover because he was swamped at work. He had surgeries scheduled all morning, was on call in the evenings, and got home too late to spend time with Abe at night. A year earlier, hell, six months earlier, he would have relieved his stress by going online and finding someone to fuck on his way home or during a lull between patients. But he couldn't do that anymore, not if he wanted to keep shooting onto Abe's tongue.

Whatever mistakes Jason had made in his life, and there had been many, having unprotected sex wasn't one of them, so he wasn't surprised when he'd gotten tested three months earlier and received an all clear. Abe was practically a virgin by Jason's standards, so, as expected, his STD tests had been negative too. After that, Jason regularly came in Abe's mouth, which turned both of them on more than Jason would have ever expected.

Abe's reaction to sucking Jason off and tasting him was the single hottest thing he had ever seen. When Abe's lips were wrapped around Jason's cock, his expression was one of complete bliss, and when Jason came, Abe moaned and whimpered, his orgasm always following almost immediately. Unwilling to lose that pleasure, Jason had stayed away from hookups, which was why he was on edge when he drove out of the hospital parking lot at nine o'clock on Friday night and called Abe.

"Hey! How was—"

"I'm on my way home," Jason snapped. "You still have my spare key, right? Meet me there."

"Oh. I was just—"

"Dammit, Abe!" Jason yelled as he tightened his fingers around the steering wheel. "I am too tired to fight right now. I've been working like a maniac all week. I almost lost a patient. I came in at six thirty this morning. It's after nine and I'm only now leaving. I've been living off cafeteria food and I haven't seen the sun in days. And despite all that, I kept my dick in my pants because if I don't, you won't swallow, so I don't think it's too much to ask you to stop whatever it is you're doing and get to my place so I can get fucking laid!"

"Okay."

The response was so quiet and mild, Jason wasn't sure he heard correctly. "Okay?" he asked, still panting from his rant.

"Come home," Abe said, and if it was possible, his voice was even softer, calmer. "I'll take care of you."

Suddenly realizing his fingers hurt, Jason loosened his grip on the wheel, peeled off one hand at a time, and stretched them, cracking his knuckles. "Okay." Jason swallowed hard as his heart rate slowed back to normal. "I'll see you soon." He cleared his throat. "Bye."

Jason ended the call and drove the rest of the way home in a daze, his muscles twitching, his head throbbing, and his jaw clenching. He wasn't sure why he was angry or even *if* he was angry. By the time he pulled into his garage, his shoulders and neck were sore and his veins thrummed with frustration at nothing and everything. After turning off his engine, he slipped his key ring over his finger, grabbed his bag, and walked into the house through the laundry room.

As he hung the keys on the new hook next to the door—another project Abe had taken care of when he stayed over—Jason realized the lights were on. He was trying to remember whether he had forgotten to turn them off when he heard soft footsteps. Swinging around toward the open door into the house, he saw Abe approaching. He was wearing a UNLV sweatshirt, tight jeans, and white socks, and before Jason could so much as say hello, he dropped to his knees, pulled down Jason's scrub pants and briefs, and took his flaccid dick into his mouth.

"Abe," Jason gasped.

"Mmm," Abe moaned quietly as he cupped Jason's balls, then rolled and squeezed them gently.

Leaning against the door to the garage, Jason closed his eyes and gave himself over to the pleasure. "Feels good, baby," he said as he combed his fingers through Abe's hair. "Missed this."

Abe continued sucking his hardening cock and caressing his balls, bringing him to full hardness in minutes.

"Gonna cum soon," Jason whispered as his nuts drew tight and his dick throbbed. Though he normally liked to stroke himself at the end of a blow job so he could control the aim of his release and paint Abe's face or lips or tongue, he didn't make a move to take over, instead letting Abe finish him off. It wasn't long before his orgasm rolled over him like a quiet wave, making his toes curl and his breath catch as he pulsed into Abe's waiting mouth.

"Feel better?" Abe asked as he stood up, sliding his body against Jason's. He pulled Jason's pants up and tucked him inside.

"Yeah." Jason opened his eyes and met Abe's concerned gaze. "Your turn," he said as he reached between them for the hard bulge behind Abe's zipper.

Shaking his head, Abe said, "Later." He wrapped his slender arms around Jason's waist and pulled him close. "You look tired. Let's eat. I made steaks and potatoes."

"Steak?" Jason said.

"Mmm-hmm." Abe brushed his hand through Jason's hair soothingly. "After the last couple of weeks you've had, you deserve to indulge, so I made red meat. We can have chicken and fish the rest of the weekend to make up for it." He kissed Jason's neck.

"Dinner's already made?" Jason asked as his brain cleared from the pleasant haze of sexual satisfaction.

"Yeah. I had everything ready and I was waiting for your call to put the steaks on. They're nice and hot."

"So you were already here making me dinner when I called?" Jason trailed his fingers down the side of Abe's face.

"Uh-huh." Abe turned and kissed Jason's palm. "I went shopping after work and stocked up for the weekend. Then I got my stuff and came here to put dinner together."

"Are you going to tell me I was out of line for yelling at you?"

"Nope." Abe put his hands on Jason's shoulders and dug into the muscle, massaging him.

"Why not?"

Sighing, Abe tipped his head back and met Jason's gaze. "Because you already know."

If that wasn't a punch to the gut, Jason didn't know what was.

"Plus," Abe continued, "I'm pretty sure I know why you were upset when you called me." Big blue eyes searched his. "Do you?"

Shrugging, Jason said, "I was horny."

"You're always horny," Abe pointed out.

"Mr. Pot, meet Mr. Kettle," Jason said.

"It wasn't an insult." Abe smiled, and the last part of the knot in Jason's gut disintegrated. "But I think there was more to it than that."

"What do you mean?" Jason furrowed his brow.

"Let's eat while the food's warm." Abe took Jason's hand in his and walked out of the room. "We can talk afterward, in the bath."

"We're taking a bath?"

"Yup. You have that big whirlpool tub you never use, and I bet you'll enjoy relaxing in the jets. I even bought bubble bath."

"I don't use it because baths make no sense. Who wants to soak in their own filth and call that getting clean?"

"Soak in their own filth?" Abe repeated slowly as he turned around.

"Yeah. Think about it. You're washing your face with the same water you're using to wash your balls."

"Hmm," Abe said. "So you're saying taking a bath with you is like cleaning your balls with my mouth? Because I have to tell you, I like doing that. I like it a lot."

"I know you do." Jason squeezed Abe's hand. "But taking a bath to get clean is like licking my own balls, which is much less appealing."

"What if we shower first so we're squeaky clean? I'll even throw in a massage."

"Deal," Jason said.

"Good." Abe turned around and leaned against the peninsula. "We'll eat dinner and then we can get in the bath and talk."

"Talk?"

Abe threw back his head and laughed.

"What?"

"We suck at this," he said. "Both of us."

Jason arched his eyebrows and curled one side of his lips up. "Oh, we both suck plenty."

"Cut it out." Abe chuckled and lightly smacked Jason's shoulder.

"Sorry." Jason cleared his throat and tried to look serious. "What do we suck at?"

"Talking."

He reared back. "We talk."

"We do," Abe agreed. "But not about everything we should."

"Fine." Jason sighed dramatically. "If you feed me and get naked and wet with me, I'm willing to suffer through a conversation."

"You really are a giver," Abe said sarcastically.

Jason arched his eyebrows, brought his fist to his mouth, and coughed.

Abe shook his head. "Is there anything you can't turn into a sexual innuendo?"

"Is there anything you can say that isn't a sexual innuendo?"

"Apparently not," Abe conceded. He ran one finger down Jason's chest, over his stomach, and across his groin. "My subconscious must see you and think sex, so everything gets tainted."

"Aww, baby, you say the sweetest things," Jason said as he stepped closer.

Abe rolled his eyes.

"You do," Jason insisted, his voice full of humor.

Abe shook his head and snorted.

Jason was amazed at how much better he felt. Less than an hour earlier, he had wanted to put his hand through a wall; now he was calm and happy. He snaked his arm around Abe's waist and brought their chests together, trapping Abe against the counter. "You do," he whispered into Abe's ear.

Trembling, Abe turned his face into Jason's neck and said, "You really do it for me."

"I know," Jason said. Abe was too earnest to play games and too inexperienced to effectively hide his emotions. His eagerness to be with Jason was evident in his every expression and action, which Jason cherished because the feeling was mutual even if he wasn't always great at showing it. "Like I said." He cupped Abe's chin, tilted his head up, and then dipped down and brushed their lips together. "The sweetest things."

"YOU WERE right about the bath," Jason said, his voice thick and his muscles relaxed.

After a delicious and filling dinner, they climbed to the third floor, which housed the master suite, and got in the shower, where

Abe washed him with painstaking tenderness. Then he left Jason to enjoy the warm spray, stepped out of the shower, and filled the separate tub for the first time in the five years Jason had owned the townhouse. When the bath was brimming with hot water and vanilla-and-lavender-scented bubbles, Abe came back and led him over. He helped Jason settle in before climbing in behind him, wrapping his legs around his torso, and massaging the tension out of every muscle in his back, shoulders, and neck.

"I haven't taken a bath since I was a kid," Abe said. He shifted slightly, and his soft nuts and cock rubbed against Jason's back.

"Mmm, me either." Jason laid his head against Abe's shoulder. "This is way better than I remember."

"It is." Abe lifted his hands and drizzled warm water onto Jason's neck and upper chest. "Are you ready to talk about earlier?"

"If I turn around and fuck you so hard you scream, will you forget about it?" That strategy had been effective on more than one occasion.

"Probably, so let's put that on hold."

Jason grunted.

"What happened?"

"Nothing," Jason said. "I was tired, hungry, stressed, and horny. Before, I would have taken care of it by going online or to a bar and hooking up. Done and done. But now I can't, so I snapped."

"And the reason you can't is because you get off on watching yourself cum in my mouth?"

"You get off on it too," Jason said defensively.

"No question about that," Abe said with a chuckle as he rocked his hips and moved his hardening dick against Jason's back. "Just talking about it revs me up." He paused. "But I don't think this was about a couple of weeks with no sex."

Making excuses to Abe was easy because Jason had been using the same ones with himself, but deep down he knew there was more on his mind than sexual frustration.

"What happened earlier?" Abe whispered as he ran his palms over Jason's chest.

With Abe's hands over his heart, he almost certainly felt Jason's heart rate speed up. "I haven't fucked anyone but you since December."

"Is that a long time for you?"

"Four months?" Jason said incredulously. "Yeah, it's a long time—it's longer than I've gone since I first fucked a guy, and I was married for most of the years since then."

"You haven't exactly been celibate during the last four months," Abe reminded him.

"I know. I'm not saying that. I'm just…."

"What?" Abe ran his lips over the perimeter of Jason's ear. "Talk to me."

"I haven't *wanted* to be with anyone else." And that was the crux of the problem. "I've seen good-looking guys and had the usual 'what does he look like naked' or 'how fast can I get him on his knees' thoughts, but nothing more than quick flashes. Nothing I've wanted to act on."

"And that scares you?"

"No," Jason said reflexively. He sighed. "Maybe. This was supposed to be a one-off."

"I remember," Abe said. "I told myself you were my birthday present. One night to be spontaneous and do whatever I wanted, repercussions be damned." Jason could hear the smile in Abe's voice. "Best present I ever got."

"It's been way more than one night."

"It has. And for me, at least, it keeps getting better the more time we spend together."

"For me too, baby." Jason covered Abe's hands with his own, tilted his head back, and kissed the bottom of Abe's chin. "But this isn't what we expected. Doesn't that scare you?"

"Well." Abe paused and silently caressed Jason's chest, presumably thinking the question over. "I guess the way I see it, whenever I start dating someone, I'm either taking the first step toward a breakup or the first step toward forever. Both of those prospects are scary, right?"

"That's just it," Jason said. "We didn't start out *dating*. It was supposed to be a hookup."

"The first time," Abe said. "It was supposed to be a hookup the first time. Maybe the second time too. But after that…." Abe let the comment trail off.

"You knew I was hoping to run into you in that coffee shop?" Jason said, suddenly realizing he hadn't been as subtle as he'd thought.

"Not at first, no. But I go to the Roasted Bean a fair bit, and when I went in one time after we met up there, a barista told me you'd asked about me."

"I wanted to see you again and I remembered you saying you went there a lot, so I thought it'd be a good place to run into you," Jason admitted.

"I'm glad."

Jason sighed. "The first step toward a breakup or the first step toward forever, huh?"

"Seems that way to me."

"After I got divorced, I stopped expecting forever," Jason said. "I didn't think it was possible for… I didn't think it was possible."

Abe's hands stilled, his body stiffened, and his voice was tense when he asked, "And now?"

"I don't know," Jason admitted, covering Abe's hand with his and twining their fingers together. "But I don't want us to break up." Of that he was absolutely certain. If anything, he wanted to see Abe more, not less. He needed Abe in his life.

With a relieved sigh, Abe said, "That's good enough."

"Okay." Jason reached for Abe's leg and caressed him. "Wait. What did we just decide?"

"I think we decided we're walking along the path and we haven't hit the fork in the road yet."

"That is way too metaphorical for me," Jason said. "How about we go with this? You want to be with me. I want to be with you. Neither of us wants to be with anybody else. So unless we tell each other it's over, we stick with that."

"Jase?"

"Yeah?"

"Did you just ask me to be in a monogamous, committed relationship with you?" Abe asked, his voice teasing.

"Quit fucking with me. It's mean. I all but had an anxiety attack earlier." It felt good to admit what happened, to himself and to Abe. Talking about it somehow made it less debilitating. Laughing about it was even better.

"Does that mean you're my boyfriend?" Abe asked liltingly.

"I'm warning you," Jason growled.

"Jason and Abe, sitting in a tree, K-I-S-S-I-N-G. First comes—"

Jason flipped around and pinned Abe to the tub.

"Jase!" he shrieked as water splashed over the edge.

"I hope you understand that I need a lot of attention," Jason said, his face hovering over Abe's. He rolled his hips, dragging his erection against Abe's thigh. They were done talking for the night. Maybe for the weekend. "This monogamy thing means you're going to be *very* busy."

Abe's pupils dilated, his cheeks flushed, and his lips reddened. "I'm counting on it," he said.

Chapter 10

"Hɪ, Kʀɪs," Abe said as he glanced at the doorway to his classroom. "Give me a minute to finish entering these grades and then we can get going."

"Okay, Mr. Green. No rush." Kris slowly walked around the room, looking at the walls and touching the edges of the books on the shelves.

"Is everything okay?" Abe asked, flicking his gaze to her.

Normally Kris was so excited about getting to the community college for her math class that she came to his room seemingly seconds after the final bell rang, breathless from running across campus, and then fidgeted impatiently until he finished whatever he was doing. She reminded him of her father in that way, although when Jason wanted something, he was less likely to fidget and more likely to demand. It was a trait that would have been off-putting if it wasn't so sexy.

"What?" She looked up at him distractedly.

"Are you okay?"

"Oh, yeah. I'm fine."

"Good." Abe smiled at her and then went back to typing. "Is the calculus class still going well?"

He was certain that question would be a surefire way to snap Kris out of whatever was distracting her and make her happy and excited. Her love for learning was second to none, and Abe could imagine her pursuing a career in academia. More than once, he had wanted to share that observation with Jason or to tell him a funny anecdote about Kris. But despite how much their relationship had solidified since their conversation a month earlier, Jason's children remained a subject wrapped in porcupine hide with a flashing "Do Not Enter" sign above it.

"Class is fine," Kris said. It was the least effusive she had ever been about the subject.

"Glad to hear it," Abe replied. Then, trying to lighten the mood, he added, "We have less than three weeks left in the school year, which means I'm busy getting everyone ready for final exams while I'm secretly planning my vacation in my head." He laughed at his own joke, making him the only person in the room who found it funny. Kris was usually a much more engaged audience. "Hmm," he said. "I must be losing my touch. I didn't even get a smile out of you."

"What?" Kris turned her head toward him and blinked in confusion.

Realizing he was dealing with something more serious than distraction, Abe shut down his computer. He'd finish entering the remaining grades at home.

"Are you meeting with the professor or any of your classmates before your class?" he asked as he shouldered his bag.

"No." Kris picked at her nail.

"Do you have homework you need to finish up?"

"Uh-uh." She shook her head. "It's all done."

Of course it was. Abe smiled and patted Kris's shoulder. "In that case, we have plenty of time before you need to be there. How do you feel about making a pit stop at my favorite coffee shop? They have good muffins and Danishes if you want a snack."

"Okay." Kris shrugged and followed him out of the classroom.

"Are you a coffee drinker or are you too young to have fallen under its spell?" Abe asked as they walked to his car.

Her father set the coffeepot every night and drank half of it before breakfast.

"I like how it smells but not the taste so much," she said.

"How about tea?" He continued making light conversation, trying to ease Kris's tension. "The Roasted Bean has a great passion fruit green tea. It's perfect for this weather."

"Okay."

Thankfully, it didn't take long for them to reach Abe's car, and then the radio eased the painful silence. They got to the coffee shop, placed their orders, and waited as the barista prepared their drinks.

"Are you okay with sitting here for a little bit while we finish our drinks?" Abe asked.

With yet another shrug, Kris picked up her iced tea and blueberry muffin.

Abe led the way to a table, sat down, and took a sip of his iced chai latte. Interfering in Jason's family's life was strictly off-limits. He didn't need to be told that to know it. After all, the only time Jason mentioned his children was to say Abe couldn't stay over on certain nights because they'd be there. But he knew Kris separately from her father, and he couldn't stand by without trying to help while a student was hurting. That she was his boyfriend's daughter made his concern more personal, but he would have reached out either way.

"I'm here if you need to talk," he said, making every effort to sound casual and nonaccusatory.

"About what?" Kris asked, looking at him measuringly.

Her expression reminded Abe of Jason, and he decided it was the eyes. Not just the brown color Kris shared with her father, but the intensity of her gaze and the shape—flat on the bottom and curved in a half-moon on top.

"Anything you need to talk about," he answered.

After only a moment's hesitation, Kris sighed and, looking relieved, said, "I'm worried about my brother."

"Why?" Abe leaned forward, his concern multiplying as he realized that in addition to Jason's daughter being upset, something was wrong with his son. "What's going on?"

"I don't know." She glanced down at her drink. "He's acting strange. I mean, he's always been a pain, but lately...."

"But lately?" Abe repeated, hoping she'd continue her thoughts.

Frowning, she said, "Lately it's more." She breathed out loudly. "He doesn't seem right."

"Have you talked to him about what's going on?" Abe asked.

"No way." Kris's eyes widened in horror and she shook her head furiously. "He'd kill me if he thought I was getting in his business."

That seemed an unusually extreme reaction, but then again, teenagers were full of extremes.

"What about your parents? Have you mentioned any of this to them?"

"My parents?" Kris said in surprise, as if the idea of talking to them had never occurred to her. "No."

"Why not? Maybe they can help."

"I don't think so. They're both busy with work. And Donny— that's my brother—is really hard on my mom. She doesn't say anything, but I see how he is. He can be scary and even though he's only thirteen, he's already bigger than me and my mom."

With every piece of information, Abe became more concerned. Hoping he wasn't crossing Jason's unspoken line etched in concrete but unwilling to ignore Kris's distress, he said, "What about your father? Maybe he can intervene."

"I don't know." Kris sighed. "We see my dad more now than we used to, but it's still kind of weird, and if we cause a lot of problems, he might not want us around as much. Donny's already making him crazy. I can tell."

Abe's heart broke, just broke. "I see," he barely managed to rasp out. "Thank you for trusting me with this." He cleared his throat. "I'll give it some thought and see if I can come up with any ideas that might help." He reached out and covered Kris's hand with his, waiting until she met his gaze before speaking again. "Do me a favor and keep an eye on your brother. If things get worse or if you think he's in real danger, let me know right away."

"Okay, Mr. Green."

He reached for his phone and started typing. "What's your phone number? I'm going to text you so you can have my number."

"You're giving me your cell number?"

Although he didn't want to make a mountain out of a molehill, he was concerned about how upset Kris was and her description of her brother's behavior. "Yes. I meant what I said. If you feel like things with your brother are dangerous, I want you to get in touch with me."

"I can call you after school hours?" she asked in surprise.

He didn't give his phone number to students. It was a horrible idea for a lot of reasons. And even with a student he knew and trusted, like Kris, it wasn't something he would normally do. But she wasn't just a student. She was Jason's daughter. And no matter how high and thick the wall Jason tried to erect between both parts of his life, Abe couldn't look at Kris without seeing the man who had captured his heart.

"Yes, you can call me after school hours. If there's a problem and your parents are at work or you're not sure what to do, you call me."

Hopefully before that happened, he'd figure out how to talk to Jason about his children without creating an explosion that registered on the Richter scale. Abe froze when he realized an adult version of a temper tantrum was his only concern. He hadn't so much as considered the possibility that Jason would walk away from their relationship if he got upset. After rethinking the situation and the possible outcomes, he came to the same conclusion—Jason might get mad at him, he might yell and stomp, but he wouldn't leave him. Not because of a bad week at work, not because of all the internal fears he was still processing, and not because Abe meddled into parts of Jason's life he wanted to keep off-limits.

Smiling to himself at that realization, Abe exchanged phone numbers with Kris and weighed his options for how to broach the topic with her father. It was Thursday, which was generally a full day at work for Jason, so he wouldn't get home until late, and they both had to work the next morning. It wasn't a good night for a difficult conversation. But Jason wasn't on call that weekend and his kids would be with their mother, so Abe would be staying at Jason's townhouse, as usual.

If he worked really fast and focused all his free time that night and the next morning on getting grades entered and the final exam prepared, he could probably leave school on Friday early enough to hit the grocery store, make one of Jason's favorite dinners, set a relaxing mood with candles and soft music, and then talk to Jason about Kris's concerns. Or he could work at a sane pace, finish the grades after school on Friday, pick up a box of chicken on the way home, and spend his energy fucking Jason into a relaxed and malleable state before dropping the unwanted conversation on him.

ABE LISTENED for the garage door and pounced the second Jason walked inside. He pinned Jason to the wall, then sucked on his neck and climbed him like a tree.

"What's gotten into you?" Jason asked breathlessly as he cupped and kneaded Abe's butt.

"I want you." Abe pressed his lips to Jason's, kissing and licking as he tugged Jason's shirt up.

"You always want me," Jason pointed out, arrogantly and accurately. "But you don't usually greet me at the door naked."

"I missed you." Abe dropped to his feet, peeled Jason's shirt off, and tossed it onto the washing machine before dropping to a squat and working on his shoes.

"Christ, baby," Jason said when Abe yanked his pants and briefs down. "Let me catch up."

"I love your dick," Abe whispered reverently as he held Jason's cock and rubbed his cheek against it. "Your balls too." He buried his face in Jason's groin, licked his testicles, and inhaled deeply. "Mmm," he moaned as the musky taste and scent took him from aroused to pulsing.

"Okay, I'm caught up," Jason said. "Damn."

Light-headed with arousal, Abe continued feasting on Jason's balls as he reached between his own legs and took himself in hand.

"I want to fuck you," Jason said, his voice strained. "Let's take this upstairs." When Abe whimpered and sucked on Jason's glans, making no move to get up, Jason tugged him to his feet. "We're going upstairs to finish this, and then you're going to tell me what got into you." He grabbed Abe's hand and hustled them out the room, Abe in tow.

"If we do it right, the answer will be you."

"What?" Jason asked.

"You said you're taking me upstairs, fucking me, and then asking what got into me," Abe reminded him. "So that'll be you. Getting into me."

"You're making jokes?" Jason said incredulously. "You get my dick so hard it's about to break off and now you're making jokes?"

The townhouse had three stories. The first was the living area—laundry room, powder room, kitchen, dining room, living room, and family room. The second, which was where Jason's kids slept, contained two bedrooms and two bathrooms. It was dark when Abe was there. And the third floor had Jason's spacious bedroom, bathroom, and closet.

"Why would it break off?" Abe asked as he reached his free hand around Jason's hip and fondled his cock. "I take really good care of it."

"Abe," Jason groaned as he bucked into Abe's palm and stumbled.

"Uh-huh," Abe said, his mouth so close to Jason's back, he knew Jason could feel his hot breath.

"Are you trying to make me lose my mind?" Jason asked, speeding up his pace as they finally reached the third-floor landing.

"If it means you're going to give me what I need, yeah."

Jason dragged Abe into the bedroom and tossed him onto the mattress. "And what is it you need?" Keeping his gaze locked on Abe's splayed form, he walked over to the nightstand, his stiff cock bobbing and reaching for his belly button.

"You," Abe rasped. He curled his fingers around his prick and gave himself friction.

"You need me?" Jason asked as he took the lube and a condom out of the nightstand. "Where?" He climbed onto the bed, knelt beside Abe, and grasped his hand. "Show me where you need me."

His palm trembling, Abe held his hand open and let Jason pour slippery liquid onto it. Though he was embarrassed about doing what Jason asked, Abe spread his legs, bent his knees, and planted his feet on the bed.

"Show me," Jason demanded again, his voice gritty and deep. He watched Abe's every movement, his dark gaze turning Abe on unbearably.

Sucking in a deep breath, Abe moved his hand between his thighs and touched his fingertips to his hole.

"That's where you need me?" Jason asked as he opened the condom and rolled it down his thick shaft.

"No," Abe answered, his throat so thick the word was almost soundless.

"Then where?" Jason knee-walked across the bed, wedged himself between Abe's legs, and looked at his pucker. "Here?" he asked, wrapping his large hand over Abe's and moving his fingers across the ridged skin.

Abe shook his head.

"No?" Jason asked, his eyes sparkling wickedly. He moved Abe's hand forward, causing him to push his fingertip into his own hole. "How about here?"

With a gasp, Abe shook his head.

Jason pressed deeper, not stopping until Abe's finger was completely buried in his ass. "What about now, baby? Is this what you need?" He pulled Abe's hand out before quickly pushing it forward again.

"Yes," Abe said, whimpering with every thrust.

"That's it," Jason rasped. "Take what you need. Fuck yourself."

"Jase." Abe shook with excitement. "Please."

"Please what?" Jason asked, his lips turned up in a knowing smirk. "You want my dick?"

He lined his finger up with Abe's, and together they plunged in and out of Abe's passage.

"Uh-huh," Abe said, rocking his hips. "Want you." He licked his lips and gazed at Jason's harsh but passionate face. Sometime over the past nine months, Jason had transformed from playing a part in an uncharacteristically spontaneous night of fun to playing front and center in Abe's erotic fantasies, daily thoughts, and hopes for the future. "Need you."

Jason scraped his fingertip over Abe's prostate, and Abe bucked, his mouth dropping open on a soundless wail. He looked into Jason's eyes as his heart pounded against his rib cage and his toes curled.

"Jase," Abe whispered.

His nostrils flaring and his lips drawn tight, Jason stared at Abe, replaced their fingers with his dick, and slowly slid inside.

"Oh God, Jase!" Abe arched his back and clutched Jason's arms. "Feels so good."

"Love hearing you," Jason said as he pressed his groin against Abe's and circled his hips. "Love every damn sound you make."

Abe's breath hitched, his eyes rolled back, and he began rocking, needing friction in his hole.

"You want to fuck yourself on me?" Jason asked, his voice gritty.

Before Abe knew what was happening, Jason pulled out, flipped Abe onto his stomach, and then shoved his dick back in.

"Ah!" Abe shouted, caught off guard by the powerful thrust.

"You want that cock?" Jason said as he slid out. "Take it." He knelt behind Abe, grasped his hips, and yanked him onto his hands and knees before impaling him once again. "Go on." Jason pushed Abe's hips forward and then pulled him back. "Fuck yourself."

His mind in a haze of lust and desire, Abe remained on all fours and began rocking, taking Jason's cock in and then groaning as it slid out. Though he moved slowly initially, before long he increased his pace until ultimately he was slamming his backside against Jason's groin.

"Yes!" Abe shouted. "Yes! Yes! Yes!"

Jason grabbed Abe's hair with one hand and his hip with the other. He dug his fingers into Abe's skin while he pulled Abe's hair. The pain intensified the experience, adding another layer, making it real. Encouraging Abe's now frantic movements, Jason yanked his hips back and pushed him forward while he tugged on Abe's hair. They grunted as their sweat-slick bodies pounded together over and over again, Jason mercilessly ravaging Abe's prostate until, with a final cry, Abe came, semen pulsing from his untouched cock.

"Fuck!" Jason yelled when Abe's body contracted around him. He pulled out, shoved Abe onto his back, whipped off the condom, and straddled Abe's heaving chest. "Fuck!" he shouted again as he stroked himself. Semen flew from his slit and splashed across Abe's neck, cheek, chin, and hair.

His gaze locked with Jason's, Abe opened his mouth.

"Oh Christ," Jason moaned raggedly. He pumped himself harder, the veins in his arms and neck straining with effort until, with a triumphant shout, he wrung a final shot of hot ejaculate onto Abe's waiting tongue.

"Mmm," Abe moaned as he swallowed and then licked his lips. "Love that taste."

Jason growled wildly. He dropped his huge frame onto Abe, tangled his fingers in Abe's hair, and licked his neck, chin, cheeks, and lips, lapping up his own seed.

With a whimper, Abe raised his hands and rubbed them along Jason's slick back.

"Abe," Jason sighed softly. He rolled onto his side, tugged Abe against his chest, and held him close. "Damn, Abe, I...." He swallowed hard, squeezed Abe tightly, and with a shaky voice whispered, "Baby."

Cuddling into Jason's warm body, Abe closed his eyes, moved his hands over whatever skin was in reach—waist, hip, thigh, back—and sighed contentedly. They lay together in comfortable silence, Jason's even breathing lulling Abe into a deeply relaxed state.

"Are you hungry?" Jason asked eventually. "We seem to have skipped dinner."

"I was at the school pretty late today, so I didn't have time to make anything, and I don't feel like getting dressed and going out." Abe wiggled closer.

"Pizza?" Jason asked.

"That's what I was thinking."

"I'll order it in a minute, but first...."

Abe tipped his head back and looked at Jason. "First?"

"First tell me what got into you." When Abe curled his lips up, Jason shook his head and said, "Other than me." He lightly pinched

Abe's backside. "Tell me what got into you other than me, you goof."

Drawing in a deep breath, Abe met Jason's gaze and said, "Kris talked to me about some problems she's having at home."

"Kris?" Jason said. "As in my daughter?"

Abe nodded.

"What kind of problems?"

"She's worried about her brother. She says he's behaving erratically."

"Donny's a teenager and he's her brother. Kristen is levelheaded most of the time, but she's still a kid, which means the two of them bicker."

"Sure. That's normal. But—" Abe bit his lip. "She's scared, Jase."

"Scared? Why? Donny's not easy to be around. I get that, but...." Jason furrowed his brow. "Scared?"

"Uh-huh."

"I don't know why she'd be scared. Maybe she was overreacting."

"Maybe," Abe conceded. "But she seemed genuinely upset, and she isn't the type to overreact."

Jason rolled onto his back but kept his arm around Abe's shoulders. He moved his hand back and forth, gently petting. "It's weird that you know my daughter enough to make that judgment."

Weighing his options carefully, Abe considered what to push. The separation Jason had in place between Abe and the rest of his life wasn't workable long-term, and now was a perfect opportunity to bring it up. Jason was relaxed, affectionate, and seemingly willing to listen. But there were more pressing issues—they needed to figure out how to help Jason's kids.

"We can talk about me knowing Kris later," Abe said. "Right now, I think we need to figure out what you're going to do about your son."

"We?" Jason said in surprise.

Despite choosing his battles, Abe ran up against Jason's line. He sighed. "I'm not asking to raise your kids." At least not yet. "But, yes, *we*. They're your children, Jase. If they're having a serious problem, that means you have a serious problem. And I hope we're at a place in our relationship where any problem of yours is a problem of mine." He searched Jason's eyes. "Are we in this together?"

"This?" Jason repeated, his eyes pinched and his forehead furrowed.

Abe flung his leg over Jason's thigh and planted his palm over Jason's heart. "Life. Are we in it together?"

It took Jason several moments to respond, but eventually he lifted Abe's hand to his mouth, kissed his wrist, and nodded. "Yes, we are." He took in a deep breath and let it out slowly. "So." He flicked his gaze to Abe's. "What are *we* going to do about Donny?"

Chapter 11

"IT REALLY is you."

At the sound of Angela's voice, Jason glanced up from his laptop. "I asked you to meet me here." He logged out of the patient charts he was reviewing, folded the screen down, and put the laptop in his bag. "Were you expecting someone else?"

She shrugged and sat across from him. "You inviting me to lunch seemed about as likely as someone getting a crack at your phone and texting me as a joke."

"Hey!" Jason said, trying to decide if he should be offended.

"Oh, please." She waved her hand dismissively. "Don't get all dramatic."

He opened his mouth to tell her off, but before he spoke, Angela said, "Do you know the last time you invited me to lunch?"

Unable to remember, he closed his mouth and reflected back.

"Don't strain yourself." Angela picked up the menu. "The answer is never." She looked at him over the top of it. "Even when we were first seeing each other, you didn't ask me out so much as we ended up places together."

That was probably true, but they'd been in school, busy with classes and activities. His instinct was to point that out, but then he worried about walking into an argument, which made him second-guess himself. Maybe he'd be better served by apologizing irrespective of whether he had a reason to be sorry. It seemed ten years of marriage had taught him something.

"Have you already ordered?" Angela asked, her attention back on the menu.

Assuming he was off the hook, Jason said, "No. I was waiting for you."

"Sorry I'm late. Patient went into labor."

"I figured."

After another minute perusing the menu, Angela set it down and said, "Okay. I know what I'm having." She looked Jason in the face. "Neither of us has time for social visits in the middle of the day, and we never see each other socially regardless of the time, so tell me why we're here."

Rubbing his palms over his eyes, Jason said, "Donny."

"What about him?"

"Don't bullshit me, Ange. What's going on?"

For a person who generally had no trouble with words, it took her a long time to respond. "Tell me what you mean."

"Are you kidding me?" Jason asked, his temper flaring. He wasn't calm on the best of days. Add in a busy work schedule, concern about the kids, and confusion about what in the hell was going on in his personal life, and he was a ticking time bomb. "Quit being cryptic and answer my damn question." He waited a few beats for her to respond, and when she didn't, he glared. "You don't have the right to keep things from me."

"Oh, is that right?" Angela snickered. "What am I keeping from you, Jason?"

"That's my question!"

Narrowing her eyes, Angela leaned forward and met his gaze. "You have complete access to the kids, to their schools, to their doctors, to every damn thing you want. When have I ever kept anything from you?"

He wouldn't argue those points because Angela was right, which put him more on edge. "Something's going on with Donny and I don't know what it is."

"And that's my fault?" Angela asked, scoffing.

"Yes! I asked a simple question and you're not answering me."

"Don't push me, Jason," she said tightly as she rubbed her fingertips over her temples.

Frustrated that wanting to know what was happening in his son's life constituted pushing, Jason yelled, "You can't keep things from me. He's my son too!"

"Then act like it!" She slammed her hands on the table.

Thankfully for everyone involved, the other restaurant patrons included, the waiter chose that moment to come and take their order.

"Caesar salad with salmon and an iced tea," Jason said, handing over the menu without looking at the waiter.

"I'll have a grilled chicken sandwich, please," Angela said. "No sprouts, but I'd like avocado if you have it, and a diet soda." When the waiter left, she sighed and said, "I'm sorry for raising my voice."

"It's fine." Jason waved her off. "Just tell me what's going on."

"Nothing that hasn't been going on for a while. Donny's angry all the time, which you already know. I wanted to take him to a therapist and he refused. I don't like it but there's nothing I can do it about it." She looked at Jason hopefully. "Maybe it's a normal teenage boy thing."

Though he hadn't ever been particularly bubbly during his teenage years, Jason didn't recall being angry to the point where he frightened people. "Kristen told Abe she's scared."

Leaning back in her chair, Angela said, "Ah, the marvelous and mysterious Mr. Green, who Kristen can't stop talking about and you refuse to mention. He works with teenagers all day. Maybe he can spend time with Donny and figure out what's going on."

Talking about his children with Abe was one thing, having them spend time together was something else entirely.

"Wow. The expression on your face just now." Angela grinned and shook her head. "That was something."

"What expression?"

"If I had to choose one description, I'd go with abject fear," she said amusedly.

Jason rolled his eyes and shook his head.

"Thank you," Angela said to the waiter who arrived with their drinks before turning her attention back to Jason. "How long have you been seeing him? I figured it out in January and it's almost June now, so that's at least"—she paused and furrowed her brow in thought—"five months?"

"Depends on when you start counting. It's been closer to ten months if you go with the first orgasm. Or maybe it was *orgasms*," Jason said, waggling his eyebrows and hoping to distract Angela from whatever point she was trying to make.

"The first orgasms?" Her eyes widened. "Wait. What's the other option?"

"What?"

"You said it's been ten months since the first time you slept with him."

"We weren't exactly sleeping."

Ignoring Jason's interruption, Angela continued talking, "But you also implied there's another measurement option."

Of the long list of reasons he hated arguing with Angela, one of the top three was that she had an uncanny ability to lead him where he didn't want to go without him knowing he was being led. "Uh...."

"Are you telling me you're with him exclusively? You're not seeing any other men at all?" she asked, even though Jason had not in fact told her that or shared any information about his personal life.

Not knowing how to respond, he stayed quiet. It was the deer-in-the-headlights approach, and he braced himself to be run over.

"That's, uh, wow." She pursed her lips in thought, arched her eyebrows, and nodded to herself. "Wow."

Rather than being grateful for the reprieve, Jason seemingly had no ability to walk away from what was sure to be a topic he'd regret. "What?" he asked. "What do you mean by that?"

Raising her hands to shoulder height, Angela said, "I'm surprised you're able to keep it up, that's all."

"I have no trouble getting it up," Jason hissed.

Angela threw her head back and laughed.

"What?" Jason said, annoyed that he kept asking the same thing and never got closer to an answer.

"Nothing," Angela said, wiping away tears at the corners of her eyes. "That was just so typical."

She kept laughing and Jason sighed. "Do you think you can finish insulting me sometime in the next few minutes so we can go back to the point of this meeting?"

"Honestly, Jason, I have no idea what you want from me," Angel said, suddenly sounding tired. She picked up her glass and sucked on the straw.

"I want to know what's going on with my kids."

"Then try spending time with your kids," she snapped.

"That's not fair!"

"Isn't it?" Angela said calmly.

The conversation was like an emotional roller coaster. Or his marriage.

She took another sip. "How often do you see them?"

"Every week."

She arched her eyebrows disbelievingly.

"Fine. I seem them at least every other week."

"And how much time do you spend with them?"

He hated answering questions that weren't really questions. "You know the answer to that."

"Yes, I do. You see them more often now than you used to, but it's still only for a night or two at a time."

"That's not true! I took them for a week."

"You took them for a week once." She set her glass down and leaned forward. "And that's the longest period of time you've spent with them consecutively, both before and after our divorce."

"That's because I have to work!" Jason said.

"So do I!"

"Dammit, Angela, it isn't the same and you know it."

"No, I don't know it. Why isn't it the same?" she asked. "Please enlighten me."

Hating to be backed into a corner, he shouted, "Because you're their mother!"

"And you're their father. Isn't that what you just said? They're your kids, and you want to know what's going on in their lives. Be a part of their damn lives and you'll see that, yes—" She raised one finger. "Donny's angry. And yes—" She raised another finger. "Kristen is scared. Who can blame her? There are times he scares me."

"Why?" Jason asked, more concerned about Angela's fear than her accusations.

"Because Kristen is my size. Donny's bigger than both of us and he's nowhere near done growing. He's five foot five and he weighs a hundred and twenty-five pounds. When he gets mad about something, he's loud and in our faces and—" she sighed. "It's not good. I don't think he'd ever actually hurt us, but his temper is frightening and I don't know how to help him." She slumped in her chair and lifted her soda, her hand trembling. "Are you happy now? You have your answers. Short of getting more involved in their lives, I don't know what you can do about any of it."

Jason picked up his glass and slowly drank, more to have something to do than because he was thirsty. When ice hit his lips, indicating that his tea was gone, he sighed and set the glass down. "I never planned to raise kids on my own," he said quietly.

"Right back at you." Angela raised her own glass in a cheer. "I never planned to have kids at all." She took another sip and then set her soda down. "But we did, two of them. The good news is neither of us is on our own. I wish you'd spend more time with them and get involved with their day-to-day lives, but that doesn't mean I want you to take them full-time."

"What *do* you want?" Jason asked tiredly. "And where the fuck is our lunch?" He looked around, hoping to catch sight of the waiter.

"I want bigger breasts, an unlimited shoe budget, and more free time."

Chuckling weakly, Jason said, "I guess I could do something about the last one."

"You could. But it's not just about me having time to breathe or go to the bathroom without interruptions." She reached out and held Jason's hand. "They want to see you more. I know they don't say it and Donny would deny it, but it's true. You're their father and they need you. Donny's probably hurting more than Kristen, but they both need you."

He had already failed as a husband. He didn't want to fail as a father. "Okay." Jason nodded, awash with concern and guilt. "I'll do better. Maybe we can make a schedule?" He looked at Angela questioningly.

"That's a good idea." She nodded. "And if they're with you, Abe will spend time with Donny and maybe he'll have some ideas about what's going on with him and how we can help."

That comment caught Jason off guard and he started coughing.

"Oh, for crying out loud." Angela threw her hands up. "Why are you so horrified at the prospect of your boyfriend meeting the kids?"

Jason shrugged and fiddled with his glass, swishing the ice around. "You don't think it's weird for children to see their father with another man?"

"Weird for who?"

"Them," Jason said as he raised his gaze.

"We've been divorced for five years, so that part isn't weird. They know you're gay, so that part isn't weird. Abe isn't a freak show who walks without moving his arms, so—"

"What?"

"What what?"

"What did you say about the arms?" Jason asked.

"This guy asked me out last week. He works in my building. Seems decent enough, pretty good-looking, but he doesn't move his arms when he walks. One time he was running to the elevator and still, nothing on the arms. I politely declined."

"You do realize you sound crazy, right?" Jason said. "Who notices what someone does with their arms?"

"Everyone notices. You just don't realize it because you take it for granted that leg motion includes arm motion. I guarantee if you saw him, you'd agree with me. It's freaky as hell. Anyway, not the point. Why do you think the kids meeting your boyfriend would be weird?"

"Christ, Ange." Jason dragged his fingers through his hair. "I don't know anymore. Maybe they should meet him. It'd make things easier given as much time as he spends at my place."

"How often does he stay at your townhouse?"

"Uh." Jason thought the question over and realized the last time Abe hadn't slept over was when the kids spent the night at his place a week earlier. The same was true for the time before that and the time before that one. He stopped going through his mental calendar. "He's with me a lot."

"I don't see any reason why that should change. If anything, I think it'll be good for the kids to see a stable relationship."

"Dear God." Jason dropped his head onto the table.

"What's wrong?"

"Did you hear yourself?" he muttered. "I'm now the role model for relationship stability. *Me.* Christ."

Angela laughed. "Okay, sit up. The waiter's coming. We don't want him to think you passed out from hunger."

"With as long as it's taken them to get the food to us, that was a real possibility."

She nodded and then smiled up at the waiter as he put their plates down. "Thank you."

"You're welcome," the waiter said. "Can I get you anything else?"

"Just refills on the drinks," Angela answered, pointing to their empty glasses.

"Sure," the waiter said. He reached for the glass just as Angela leaned forward to get her napkin, and his arm made contact with her chest. "Pardon me." His cheeks turned red. "I'll be right back with your drinks."

After the guy scurried away, Jason leaned forward and whispered conspiratorially, "I think he likes you."

"He's cute, but I don't have time to date," Angela said as she lifted the bun and removed half the lettuce from her sandwich.

Jason flinched, realizing he was at fault for part of that. "We'll make a schedule and I'll take the kids half the time."

"Half?" Angela asked in surprise. "You'd really do that?"

Damn, he was an ass. Angela was right. Kids needed their fathers. "Yes, really. I'll talk to Abe and see if he's willing to stick around for it."

"You think he'd break up with you because you want to spend more time with your kids?"

The idea hadn't even crossed Jason's mind. "No." He shook his head. "That isn't what I meant." He picked up his fork and speared a piece of salmon. "Abe wouldn't leave me. I just don't know if he'll want to stay at his apartment when the kids are over or if he'll want to keep staying with me."

"Okay," Angela said quietly. They ate in silence for a few moments, and then she said, "Jason?"

He stuffed a bite of salad into his mouth. "Yeah?"

"In case you listen to the words that come out of your mouth as well as you listen to what comes out of mine, which is to say not well, I'll point out that you just said the man you've been seeing would never leave you."

His fork halfway to his mouth, Jason froze. That was exactly what he'd said, and he'd meant every word.

"Like it or not, you just confirmed your status as the stable-relationship role model," Angela said.

"That's disturbing." He had no earthly idea how or when it happened, though he supposed the lack of drive to fuck other guys should have been a decent clue about the latter.

"I agree." Angela took a bite of her sandwich. "I didn't see it coming, but I guess it makes sense if I think about it. You always were big on family."

"I was a horrible husband. What makes sense about me being a role model for healthy relationships?"

"You weren't a horrible husband, just an unfaithful one." She lifted the bun, took off a tomato, and chewed on it. "Maybe you've turned a corner."

More like spun in mental circles. "Well, now that you'll have more time to yourself, you can start dating," Jason said. "Maybe the no-arm-movement guy is still interested."

"I've spent the last fifteen years focused on other people, and you think I'll take what little free time I can get and spend it on someone else?" She shook her head. "No way. I don't need a date. I want to read a book or take a bath or maybe learn pottery." She sighed wistfully. "There's a woman in my office who makes lovely vases. I wonder if there's room in the studio where she takes classes."

"Sounds like no-arm-movement guy is out of luck."

She nodded and continued eating her lunch.

"It's sad," Jason said. "With his condition, getting a date seems particularly critical."

"His condition?"

"If he can't get good range of motion in either arm and nobody will help him out, how's he supposed to—" Jason raised his hand and moved it up and down in a mimic of masturbation.

Nearly choking on her food, Angela coughed, pulled the straw out of her glass, and gulped her soda. "You're horrible," she said. But she was smiling and laughing, so he knew their earlier disagreement was over and he'd been forgiven.

"Ange?"

"Yes?"

"Thank you for"—the list was too ridiculously long to name, and he had no idea where to start—"everything."

"You're welcome."

Satisfied with the resolution, Jason focused on his food.

"So," Angela said.

Looking up from his plate warily, Jason said, "What?"

"I know you don't have range of motion issues, but is your, uh, boyfriend taking care of your needs well?"

"Are you asking me about my sex life?"

"Hey, you introduced the topic," she said, waving a french fry around.

"In a general joking sort of way. Not as part of an actual conversation."

"So, what? You're shy all of a sudden? Those pictures I used to find on your phone were the furthest thing possible from a shy courtship."

Wincing at the memory of Angela holding up his phone and yelling about the chats he'd had setting up places and times to meet men for a quick fuck, Jason looked down at his plate.

"Okay, fine." She sighed. "I thought maybe we'd gotten there, but I see we haven't."

"Gotten where?" Jason asked hesitantly.

She took a bite of her sandwich, wiped the sides of her lips with her napkin, and said, "Friendship."

"We're friends," Jason said in surprise. "We've always been friends."

"I know. I know. But I meant *friends* friends, you know?"

"Uh, no, I don't."

"Our friendship is amazing in the land of Divorceville, but it's not like we talk as openly as I do with my girlfriends."

"That's because I'm a man," Jason pointed out.

"Which means that you can't manage to string a sentence together or that you don't have sex?"

"Do you have a point or are you insulting me for sport again?"

"I never insult you for sport," she denied.

Jason arched his eyebrows skeptically and popped a piece of salmon into his mouth.

"I don't," she insisted. "It's just a happy little side effect of most of our conversations."

"If your goal is to get me to talk more rather than less, you're moving in the wrong direction."

"Forget it." Angela picked at the bun. "I'm fine with our awesome divorce friendship."

Saying she was fine meant she wasn't fine. That was one of the first things Jason had learned as a married man. Normally, he would have waited for the topic to change or for Angela to bounce back and move on. But after their discussion that day, he realized he owed her more than he could repay. She had been raising his children essentially on her own for five years. Who was he kidding? She had been raising them essentially on her own since they were born.

"Why do you want to hear about my sex life?" Jason asked resignedly.

"Because it's important to you." Angela looked at him, her gaze full of sincerity. "I don't know if we would have ended up getting married if I hadn't gotten pregnant, but I like to think we would have stayed friends and then you wouldn't have had to hide so much and maybe...." She sighed. "We used to laugh together all the time, remember? And we told each other about problems with classes and with our families. You confided in me about things that mattered."

He considered what she said for a few moments and then forced himself to set aside his well-honed habit of deflecting and hiding. "Since December, my sex life has been pretty different." He cleared his throat. "That's when things got more"—he tried to think of the right word—"stable with Abe."

"Different how?" Angela asked interestedly. "Less exciting?"

"No." Jason thought about Abe begging for him, riding him, sucking him down. His dick hardened and his breath caught. "It's plenty exciting. I meant it's been different for me to be with the same guy and nobody else."

Nodding, Angela said, "Do you like it?"

Jason pondered that question. "I like it with Abe. I'm not sure if it'd work for me with someone else, but the two of us…. We fit really well together." He tried to think of words Angela would understand. "I'm insanely attracted to him. I like being around him. He makes me feel good. And he puts up with my bullshit without being a doormat."

Angela raised her glass in a silent toast. "More power to him. Living with a doctor is hard enough. A surgeon's even worse. With you it's—" She shuddered and shook her head.

"You're insulting me again," Jason pointed out. "And he doesn't live with me."

She smirked.

Ignoring her, the clothes that occupied previously empty portions of his closet, and Abe's toiletries in his bathroom, he said, "Anyway, it's good with him. Really good." He grinned at Angela and waggled his eyebrows. "And the sex is off the fucking charts."

"Really?" She leaned forward. "Tell me everything. I haven't gotten any in way too long."

"Why not?" he asked. "You're gorgeous. You're smart. And you're not living with a gay guy who sucks in the sack anymore."

"You didn't suck."

Jason looked at her levelly.

"Okay, fine. The sex was horrible. I thought you were allergic to foreplay and suffered from ED before I realized what was really going on. Seriously, who's ever heard of a guy saying he's too tired or has a headache? And how did you get through human anatomy without having a clue about where to find my—"

"Point made." Jason held up his hand in a "stop" motion. "You don't need to list all my shortcomings and destroy my fragile ego."

"Your ego is the last thing from fragile, but whatever. I don't care." She rubbed her palms together. "Give me dirt."

"This is a little pathetic," Jason said. "You need to get laid."

"I have two children, a busy job, and no desire to spend my life catering to another man."

"You don't have to spend your life doing anything. I'm talking about sex, not getting married. Go out, get drunk, and find someone to screw."

"I'm not the bar-hopping, bed-hopping type." She scrunched her nose and apologetically said, "No offense."

"None taken." Both because he didn't think there was anything wrong with bar hopping or bed hopping and because he no longer did either. "Fine. If you want details, I'll give you details. At the very least, I can improve my reputation as a bad lay."

"Sure. If that's what you need to tell yourself," she said animatedly. "Now spill."

Chapter 12

"HI." ABE glanced over his shoulder and smiled at Jason before turning back to the grill pan in front of him. "How was your day?"

"My day was good." Jason walked over to Abe, caressed his backside, and then kissed his neck while he rubbed his hip. "Work was work." Jason pressed his face into Abe's hair, inhaled deeply, and then sighed contentedly before stepping away. "I had lunch with Angela."

That got Abe's attention. "Did you talk about Donny? Do you know what's going on with him?"

"We did and I don't." Jason scratched the back of his head and opened the refrigerator. "Do you want a beer?"

"I'm good with water." Abe tilted his chin toward the glass next to him.

"Okay." Jason picked up a beer bottle, twisted the cap off, and closed the refrigerator with his hip. "Angela said she's noticed Donny's anger issues, but he won't go to therapy and she doesn't know what's wrong with him." He walked to the tall stainless-steel trash can, stepped on the foot pedal, and flipped the bottle cap inside. "She seemed exhausted."

Abe nodded, chewed on his lip, and knit his eyebrows in thought. He had to tread carefully around this subject, but he couldn't ignore it. He'd seen too many students make bad choices that led to more bad choices that led to destroyed lives. He wouldn't let that happen to Jason's family.

"I've never met your son and I hope I'm not overstepping." Abe scratched his calf with his socked foot, picked the chicken breasts up with the tongs, and flipped them over. "But that doesn't sound good and I'm worried it's going to get worse."

"So am I." Jason dragged one hand through his black hair, tilted his bottle against his lips, and swallowed down amber liquid. "What kind of help do you need with dinner?" he asked as he flicked his gaze around the kitchen.

"Nothing. I put one of those bagged salads together." He tilted his head toward a bowl on the peninsula. "And made rice pilaf." He pointed his chin toward a saucepan on the stove. "The chicken's done, so I just need to plate everything." When Jason headed toward the cabinet with the dishes, Abe said, "I'll take care of it. You've had a rough day. Go sit down." He flipped off the burner and had started moving toward the cabinet when he met Jason's gaze.

Tired, Abe recognized. Jason worked hard all week, and by Friday, he was generally exhausted. Worry made sense in light of the situation with his children. But it was the pained longing that took his breath away.

"Jase?" he rasped.

With a strained moan, Jason stepped over to him and swept him into a tight hug. He hunched down, curling his large frame around Abe and burying his face in Abe's neck.

"What's wrong?" Abe asked. He raised his hand and brushed it through Jason's hair. "Is this about your son?"

"Yes," Jason said, the word muffled by Abe's skin. "No." He shook his head. "Christ. I'm not making any sense." He chuckled humorlessly. "I don't want to be a fuckup anymore."

"You're not a fuckup. You're a successful doctor. You have a great house and a fancy car. You—"

Jason pulled away and walked toward the counter, his back to Abe. "I was too scared to admit I was gay, so I tried to avoid it and got Angela pregnant, which totally messed up the life she had planned. Then I guilted her into marrying me, talked her into having another kid, and didn't do anything to help her with either of them.

And after all of that, I screwed up my marriage because getting off was more important to me than keeping my vows and giving my children a stable home. Now Angela looks ready to drop and my kids are angry and scared." He set his beer bottle on the counter, sucked in a deep breath, and turned around to face Abe. "How's that for being a fuckup?"

Not sure how to respond, Abe did the only thing he could think of—he rushed forward, wrapped his arms around Jason's waist, and held on tightly.

"I can't keep going like this," Jason whispered. "They're my responsibility, my family."

Sighing in relief, Abe said, "Good."

"Do you understand what I'm saying?" Jason asked. He tugged Abe's hair until Abe tilted his head back and met his gaze. "They need more of my attention. I told Ange I'm going to take them half the time." He licked his lips. "We haven't figured out all the details yet, but they'll probably be here every other week or something like that."

They were at a turning point moment in their relationship, and even though Abe should have seen it coming, he was wholly unprepared. Resting his cheek against Jason's chest, he lowered his gaze and said, "You don't want me to come over as much."

"No," Jason said. "That's not true. Abe, I...." He cleared his throat. "Knowing you're here when I get home makes this place feel like home. I love being with you."

"Then what are you saying?" Abe looked up and searched Jason's eyes. "Tell me what you want."

"What I want?"

Abe nodded but didn't speak. He knew what he wanted, but there wasn't anything else to say until he heard the answer to his question.

"I'm not sure it matters," Jason said.

"It matters to me."

Stepping away, Jason rubbed his hand over his nape. "I'm trying not to be selfish here, baby." He walked to the refrigerator, paced across the kitchen to the sink, and then returned. "Damn, Angela would love this." He tilted his head back and closed his eyes. "Even when I try not to make it about me, that's what it comes down to."

"I'm lost," Abe admitted.

Jason stopped, turned toward the counter, and grabbed it with both hands. "Angela asked me about you."

Trying not to get winded from the change in topic, Abe said, "What did she want to know?"

Jason's knuckles whitened, and he rolled his head from shoulder to shoulder. "A lot of things, but one was whether you'll break up with me if the kids are around more."

"What?" Abe asked in horror. "I hope you told her I wouldn't do that."

"That's what I said." Jason nodded. "But later I got to thinking and—" He swallowed hard. "You can do better than me."

"No, Jase, what—"

"You're younger, better-looking, nicer." Jason squeezed his eyes shut and shook his head. "What the fuck are you doing with a guy who's closer to forty than he is to thirty, works all the time, has a bad temper, and to top it all off, has children with personal problems who need attention?"

"Tell me this," Abe said, trying to keep his voice steady. "Do you want me to leave?"

"You *should* leave." Jason slumped, curling in on himself. "I'd fucking run from me so fast I'd leave scorch marks on the ground."

"That's not what I'm asking." Though Abe wanted to go to Jason, to comfort him, he didn't for fear of being turned away. As it was, he worried about losing control of his emotions, something he doubted Jason would welcome. "Do you *want* me to leave?"

"Why would I want you to leave?" Jason said after several moments of silence. "Nobody would want that." He straightened his posture and ran his gaze up and down Abe's body. "You're a wet dream come to life. The sweetest, most patient man on earth, like a damn angel. Until the clothes come off, and then you're filthy and sexy and so damn horny you make my balls ache." He rubbed his palms over his eyes. "Christ. You'd tempt a monk, Abe, and I'm about the furthest thing possible from one. No, I don't want you to leave, but why on earth would you want to stay?"

Blinking back tears of happiness at Jason's odd rendition of sweetness, but aching for the loneliness he saw beneath it, Abe took a step toward him and smiled. "Well." He cleared his throat and closed the distance between them, stopping when he stood a couple of inches away. "You're amazing in bed and you're loaded."

It took Jason a second to process that statement, and then he smiled from ear to ear. "Both very true observations." He opened his arms, and Abe could see hope blossoming in his expression. "So you'll keep coming around, even when my kids are here?"

"Yes." Abe stepped into Jason's embrace. "And I'm really looking forward to meeting your son. I already adore Kris."

"Well, she takes after her mother. Donny, unfortunately, exhibits more of my characteristics."

"Then he'll probably win me over right away, just like his father."

"I have no idea how I did that," Jason admitted. He brushed his lips over Abe's forehead. "Now that I know you, I wonder why you ever agreed to talk to me, let alone take me home with you."

"I already told you." Abe nudged Jason's chin up with his nose and then sucked on his neck. "You're great in bed and you have lots of money."

"You said I was *amazing* in bed, but the most I've done for you with my money is bought a few dinners out. If being a kept man is your goal, you're not getting very far."

Shrugging, Abe said, "Maybe the sex is just that good." He gazed at Jason's rugged, masculine features and traced his strong jawline with the back of his hand. "Or maybe I genuinely like you. Maybe I'm drawn by your intelligence and dedication to your work, your spicy, passionate temper, and your commitment to your family and desire to be a good father."

"That's—" Jason cleared his throat. "That's harder to live up to than making a lot of money and worshiping you in bed."

"Somehow I don't think you'll have trouble with any of those." Abe combed his fingers through Jason's hair and gazed into his dark, intelligent eyes. The intensity of the moment ramped up until Abe had trouble filling his lungs. Needing a way to release the desire and emotion that filled him, he said, "But if you're worried about it, you can give me a demonstration of that worshiping part."

"Gladly." Jason slanted his mouth over Abe's and flicked his tongue across Abe's lips, waiting for Abe to part them before sliding inside. "Love how you taste." He wound his arms around Abe's hips and grabbed his butt, digging his fingers into the muscle. "Hold on, baby," Jason said as he lifted Abe. He set him on the counter, wedged himself between his spread knees, and cupped both sides of his face. "You're so beautiful." He slid his palms across Abe's temples to his nape while he lowered his open mouth to Abe's and kissed him again.

With a whimper, Abe wrapped his legs around Jason's waist and clutched his shirt. They slid their tongues together, tasting and connecting, as they tenderly touched each other.

"Mmm," Jason moaned. He dragged his open lips over Abe's, scraping with his tongue and teeth until Abe felt like he was being eaten, consumed. "We won't be able to do this when my kids are here," Jason whispered. He kissed Abe and bit his lower lip.

"Not in the kitchen, but your bedroom is on a different floor and this place is really well insulated," Abe pointed out. He dragged his hand down Jason's flank and shivered at the heat generated from that big body. "We'll be fine."

Jason rested his forehead against Abe's and exhaled. "You know what you said about me being a good father isn't true. I always wanted a family, but I haven't been there for them."

"Hopefully you're being too hard on yourself, but even if you're right, it's not too late." Abe circled his finger over Jason's nipple through his shirt. "Like you said, they need you. You can be there for them now."

Nodding, Jason ran his thumb over Abe's lower lip and gazed into his eyes. "I hope so. I want to be." He leaned forward and brushed his lips over Abe's. "When do you want to meet them?"

They were both fully dressed. Abe was sitting on the kitchen counter. Jason was standing in front of him. They were quietly talking. And yet it was one of the most profoundly loving moments of Abe's life. He was being included, not only in Jason's bed or his home, but in his family, his life.

"Do they know you've been seeing someone?"

"Angela does, but not the kids." Jason shook his head. "No."

Pinching Jason's nipple, Abe said, "But they know that one day, when you find someone, it'll be a man?" He ran his thumb over the swollen bud soothingly.

"They know I'm gay," Jason said. "Until I met you, I never thought in terms of being with someone for anything other than sex, and Angela doesn't date at all, so I have no idea what my kids expect as far as their parents and relationships."

"Well, in that case, it might be a little awkward." Abe focused on the other nipple, pinching and pulling through the fabric, his mouth watering at the thought of sucking on it. "But it has to happen sooner or later, right?"

"I don't know about that, but I want you in my life, so it *is* happening." Jason petted the back of Abe's head tenderly and kissed his cheek. "At this point, it's only a matter of working out the details."

Sighing, Abe tightened his legs around Jason's waist and wrapped his arms around his neck, holding on in every way he could. This was it—his forever man, his forever family. They hadn't said all the words and he was sure the road ahead would be rocky, but Jason was letting him in, which told him all he needed to know.

"We've got two weeks left before school gets out." He rested his head on Jason's shoulder and licked his neck. "Summer break will be a good time to make changes, because the kids can adjust without impacting their schoolwork."

"Good point," Jason said. He squeezed Abe and then lifted him off the counter and set him on the floor. "Let's eat before everything gets cold. I'll call Ange after dinner and run that plan by her."

"HONESTLY, I don't know how you guys get by without purses," Angela said as she dug through her bag.

"We throw away our receipts." Jason tilted his head toward the pile of tiny papers Angela was assembling on the table. "And our, uh...." He leaned forward. "Are those pills?"

"Mints," Angela said, flicking her gaze toward the tiny white ovals nestled with the receipts. "And maybe antacids." She put a handful of small laminated cards on the table and glanced up at Abe, who was sitting across from her. "Customer cards for grocery stores and drug stores. They never stay tucked into the slots in my wallet, so they end up in the bottom of my purse."

"I think you can type your phone number into the credit card machine at the store and get the discounts without having the actual cards."

"Really?" she asked, arching her eyebrows.

Abe nodded.

"Great. I'll toss them and then maybe I'll be able to close my wallet." She pushed the laminated cards into the growing pile of receipts and pills.

"Christ, Ange, how much are you shopping?"

"I like shoes." She shrugged and continued emptying her purse. "And coffee. And jewelry."

"And underwear," Abe said, trying not to laugh as Angela set a pair of purple lace panties on the table.

"Angela!" Jason hissed. "We are in a restaurant."

"It's more of a bar. Besides, they're clean," she said distractedly. "Aha! I knew I had ChapStick in here!" She pulled a blue stick out of her purse and held it up victoriously. "Mmm," she said as she ran it over her mouth. "That's better." She smacked her lips together and dropped the ChapStick back in her purse. "So, what were we talking about?" She looked back and forth between Jason and Abe.

"Nothing. You sat down, said hello, and then"—Jason pointed at the stack of miscellaneous items—"did that."

"I'll throw it out." Angela rolled her eyes and reached for the trash. "Oh, I need this button." She rescued a small Ziploc bag holding a brown button from the pile and dropped it into her purse.

"Don't forget your underwear," Abe said with a chuckle.

"Right. They're new." She put the purple lace in the purse and then scooped up the remaining trash and stood up. "Be right back."

"I already love her," Abe said, watching Angela walk toward the restroom. "She's awesome."

"Here." Jason shoved his keys toward Abe. "With the way things are going, you'll have to drive us home. I plan to drink liberally for medicinal purposes."

Chuckling, Abe squeezed Jason's thigh. He put the keys next to his wallet and met the waiter's gaze from a few tables over. "If you know what Angela wants, we can order now." Just then, he saw Angela returning to the table. "Never mind. Here she comes."

"Thank Christ."

The waiter and Angela arrived at the same time. "I'll have a white wine," she said.

"Beer for me," Jason said. "You have Dos Equis on tap, right?" The waiter nodded and Jason continued, "And some chips and salsa."

"And guacamole," Angela said.

"I'm good with water for now." Abe smiled at the waiter.

Once he left, Angela looked at Abe. "You can't imagine how hard it was for me to come meet you without telling Kristen. If she knew I was having dinner with the famous Mr. Green, she would have stowed away in the back of the car."

"Is she watching your son?"

"Donny's sleeping over at a friend's house, which is good because he says he's too old for a sitter and he refuses to answer to his sister."

"He's thirteen?" Abe asked.

"Yes. His birthday's in September. The 29th."

Abe nodded but wasn't sure what else to say. It seemed he wasn't alone in that condition, because the table fell silent.

After a couple of minutes, Angela leaned forward and said, "Abe." She paused. "I can call you Abe, right? Because now that you're part of the family, Mr. Green would be weird."

Bracing himself for Jason to dispute that statement or otherwise react unfavorably, Abe tensed, but when nobody spoke, he regained his composure and said, "Yes, please call me Abe."

"Abe, I agree with your suggestion about starting the new schedule once school gets out." She looked at Jason. "And every other week is fine with me." She cleared her throat. "What's your plan for introducing the children to Abe?"

"I hadn't thought about it," Jason said.

With a shake of her head, Angela turned to Abe.

"How about this?" Abe said to Jason. "We'll pick an evening for them to come over. I won't be there, so you can talk to them privately. And then when you're ready for me to come home, you can text me. I'll pick up pizza and ice cream."

"Food bribery. I like it," Angela said. "Next Saturday?"

Abe looked at Jason. "Jase?"

"It's a good plan." He wrapped his arm around Abe's back and squeezed his nape affectionately. "Thank you."

"You're welcome." Abe met Jason's gaze and smiled at him. "I'm glad you're letting me do this."

"I'm glad you want to." He leaned closer and whispered, "I'm not sure I could handle it alone."

"You could," Abe assured him, tipping his head to the side and brushing it against Jason's shoulder. "But you won't have to."

Jason wouldn't be alone if it was up to Abe. Neither of them would.

Chapter 13

IMPLEMENTATION OF Abe's plan had gone about as expected. Kristen had been excited beyond words that Abe would be a bigger part of her life, and Donny had essentially ignored everyone and everything they said.

The week that followed had been busy with Jason acclimating to having the children around for a longer period of time, the kids learning the ropes at the activities and classes they were attending for the summer, and Abe trying to make everyone comfortable with the new arrangement. By the time the kids left for their week at Angela's house, Jason was exhausted, ready for a break, and worried about Abe. Changing everything about his life for his own children was hard enough; no way would he do it for someone else's kids. And he worried Abe would come to the same conclusion and decide the hassle wasn't worthwhile.

But, remarkably, Abe hadn't complained at all, and now it was Friday and they were embarking on another week with the kids. Because Abe was off work for the summer, he had done the majority of the driving and picking up the last time they'd had the kids. He said he'd be able to do it again, but he suggested that Jason pick them up the first day and have some time alone with them in case there was anything they wanted to talk about with just him.

So Jason forced himself to roll out of bed before the sun rose, wanting to go into work early to make up for the time he'd

lose at the end of the day. He inadvertently moved the comforter
when he got up, leaving Abe exposed to the cool air in the room,
so he took hold of it and turned back to the bed, intending to
cover Abe. The sight that greeted him—Abe lying facedown, his
arms curled underneath him, completely nude—made him lose
focus on his plan.

Before he consciously realized what he was doing, Jason
climbed back onto the bed and blanketed Abe's nude body with his
own, needing the skin-to-skin contact. The scent of Abe's skin
predictably turned him on, and he began laying openmouthed kisses
across his shoulder blades and nape.

"Mmm, Jase," Abe moaned. He raised his head without
opening his eyes, and Jason skated his lips over Abe's cheek and
eyebrow.

"Good morning, baby."

Abe smiled and thickly mumbled, "Good morning." He
straightened his right arm, reached back, and ran his palm over
Jason's hip. "You feel good."

Flicking his tongue over Abe's skin with every kiss, Jason
continued worshiping the smooth, warm body beneath him as he
blindly reached toward the nightstand. "Sorry for waking you," he
said as he grabbed the condoms.

"That's okay." Abe leaned up and turned his face, meeting
Jason's lips for a kiss. "I can sleep more after you go to work."

"What do you have going on today?" Jason planted his left
hand on the bed, pushed himself up, and ripped the condom wrapper
open with his teeth.

"I'm going grocery shopping to get snacks for the kids,
meeting my friends for lunch, and then helping one of them pack
and move."

"That sounds nice." Jason nipped the curve of Abe's ear as he
rolled the condom onto his swollen shaft. "The condom's
prelubricated. Do you need more?"

"No, I'm good." Abe shook his head and tilted his ass up. "Just
go slow."

Jason slid between Abe's legs, parted his cheeks, and rubbed
his cock over Abe's cleft while he kissed and licked his back.

"Ungh," Abe moaned, and he tensed as Jason slid his thick shaft inside the small, tight hole. When Jason fully breached the welcoming passage, Abe sighed in pleasure. "Yes," he whispered.

"Love how hot and tight you are inside." Jason rocked in and out, all the while brushing his lips over whatever part of Abe he could reach.

They moved in concert, hips connecting and parting through the gentle joining, both of them moaning softly. When the need for more pressure and speed became too intense to ignore, Jason slipped his arms under Abe's, grasped Abe's shoulders, and held on tightly while he pumped his hips.

"Fuck. Yes. Love this." Jason dragged his teeth over Abe's nape and tugged on his skin. "Uh, uh, uh," he grunted his way through the pleasure, holding Abe immobile as he thrust inside one last time and spilled long and deep.

Giving himself a few seconds to catch his breath, Jason trembled and gnawed on Abe's shoulder before gently pulling out. He urged Abe onto his back and then crouched over him and took Abe's hard, pink shaft into his mouth.

"Jase!" Abe cried out. He undulated his hips while Jason licked and sucked on his cock, and before long, Abe moaned in satisfaction and pulsed thick streams of ejaculate into Jason's mouth.

"Christ." Jason kissed Abe's belly. "I want to skip work and stay in bed with you all day."

"We'll do that next weekend." Abe combed his fingers through Jason's hair and massaged his scalp.

"Okay," Jason said with a deep sigh as he sat up. He pulled off the condom, got out of bed, and kissed Abe's forehead. "Go back to sleep. I'll see you after work." Jason grabbed the wayward comforter off the floor and laid it over Abe, who was already closing his eyes.

HOLDING UP his iPhone, Donny called out to his sister, "Hey, Kris. I just asked Siri if she has any advice for you, and she said the clown makeup and slutty clothes aren't enough to get a guy interested."

Though she stumbled, the distraction was only momentary, and then Kristen ignored her brother, who was sprawled across the couch in the family room, and walked into the kitchen, where Jason was working on dinner. "Where's Mr. Gree—uh, Abe?" she asked. "Isn't he going to eat with us?"

"Abe is helping a friend pack and move," Jason said in response to Kristen's question. "But he should be home soon." He looked at his daughter appraisingly and said, "That's not what you were wearing when I picked you up, is it?"

Though he rarely paid attention to clothing, he was pretty sure Kristen hadn't been wearing a short, tight dress when she got into his car in front of the community college. Donny was training as a junior lifeguard at the country club where Angela had a membership. But Kristen had forgone the opportunity for mindless fun and instead signed up for a full slot of summer classes.

"Nuh-uh." She shook her head and wandered over to the refrigerator. "I changed." She stood in front of the open door but didn't reach for anything inside. "So he's on his way now?"

Taking another careful look at his daughter's clothing, Jason thought about her question and Angela's comments that Kristen spoke about Abe often and glowingly. Generally, he felt nauseous at the prospect of his daughter dating or having any interactions with males, so he avoided discussing it at all costs. But he couldn't ignore the possibility that she had a crush on Abe. It would make their already stressful life painfully awkward for everyone.

Gathering up his nerves, Jason said, "Kristen, there's no easy way for me to ask this." He cleared his throat and stirred the pot of water. He was waiting for it to boil so he could add spaghetti to it, but for now it was just water, which didn't require stirring. Needing something to do with his hands, he stirred anyway. "But did you get dressed up to impress Abe?"

"Why would I—" Kristen gasped. "Dad! No. Gross. Mr. Green is old!"

"Old?" Jason looked over his shoulder at her. "He's twenty-six, almost twenty-seven." Which made Abe a little more than eleven years older than Kristen, who was fifteen, and a little less than eleven years younger than Jason, who would be turning thirty-seven on July 31, which was only a month away. The calculation made his already queasy stomach lurch.

"Well, he seems old and he's my teacher!" She slammed the refrigerator shut and stomped over to the pantry. "That's gross."

"Hi, guys," Abe called out as the laundry room door opened. "I brought donuts." He walked into the kitchen and set a large pink box on the peninsula.

Apparently having seen the box, Donny rushed over and grabbed it.

Wanting to avoid an argument about eating dessert before dinner, Jason tried to compromise. "How about you eat half of one now and finish it after dinner?"

Before Jason could get a knife from the drawer, Donny had the box open and he was eating a glazed donut with chocolate frosting ripped in half. "This is good," he said through a mouthful of pastry as he walked back to the family room, carrying the box.

"Now I know to pick up Ronald's when I want to get on Donny's good side." Abe stepped over to Jason and met his gaze. "Hi," he said softly, his tone and the sparkle in his eyes saying much more than hello. "How was your day?"

"Good." Jason turned away from the stove and brushed his thigh against Abe's leg, needing the connection, however slight. "How was yours?"

"Fine. I'm glad to be home." Abe caressed Jason's arm, sighed contentedly, and then smiled at Kristen, who was fidgeting in front of the pantry. "Hi, Kris. Is that a new dress?"

"It's a hand-me-down from my mom. It was too small, so she said I could have it."

Jason snorted and laughed into his hand.

Abe gave him a look that was equal parts amused and scolding and then stepped away. "Are you making spaghetti? There're meatballs in the freezer. We can heat them in sauce and they'll be ready to go."

"Yup," Jason said.

"Kris, the jars of sauce are on the second shelf in the pantry. Will you get two?" Abe said as he walked to the refrigerator.

"Sure." She paused. "Do you think my dress looks okay?"

Abe turned back around and gave her his attention. "Yes. Do you have plans tonight?"

"No," Jason said at the same time Kristen said, "Yes."

"What plans?" Jason asked her. "You didn't say anything about plans."

"I, uh, thought I should wait for Abe to get home first."

"Why?" Jason asked.

When Kristen didn't answer, Jason glanced at Abe, who looked similarly confused for a moment, and then his expression changed into amusement.

"Jase, I think maybe Kristen has a date."

"What?" Jason said, more loudly than he had intended. "You're too young to date!"

"I'm fifteen and a half."

"Which is too young to date," Jason insisted.

"In 1953, maybe." She rolled her eyes and whined, "Dad."

"No. Absolutely not."

"Abe," Kristen pleaded. "Will you please talk to him?"

"There's nothing to talk about," Jason said. "Putting on makeup and clothes might make you look older, but you're still a kid and you're not going out with boys."

"Kris, you can watch the water and put the pasta in when it boils, right?" Abe set a bag of frozen meatballs on the counter.

"Yes," Kristen said.

"Good." Abe walked over to Jason and lightly clasped his wrist. "Come upstairs with me."

"Why? This isn't up for discu—"

Abe leaned forward, getting close enough to kiss but not actually making contact. "You're still wearing your work clothes. I thought you'd want to change."

"These aren't the scrubs I wore in the OR this morning. I changed into them before rounds in the afternoon."

Abe dropped his gaze to Jason's mouth and then up to his eyes. Jason took in a deep breath and reminded himself that sporting an erection in scrubs was almost impossible to conceal. "But, yeah, that's a good idea. I should change," he said. "And I, uh, need to take a quick shower too."

"Kris, can you put the sauce in a pan on low with the meatballs?" Abe asked as he followed Jason out of the kitchen.

Kristen nodded. "Sure."

They walked toward the staircase, and Jason noticed Donny eating a strawberry-glazed donut. "That's the last donut," he said. "I don't want you to spoil your dinner."

"He has headphones in," Abe said when Donny didn't respond.

"Something tells me he wouldn't answer even if he could hear me." Jason stomped over to Donny and pulled one of the speakers out of his ear. "That's the last donut until after dinner."

Donny rolled his eyes, replaced his earbud, and looked at his phone as he continued chewing.

"We were going upstairs, remember?" Abe said as he caressed Jason's hip.

Abe was close enough for Jason to breathe in his scent, which reminded him of the reason they were going to the bedroom. "Let's go," Jason said.

They hustled up the stairs, and he managed to keep himself in check until they were in the bedroom with the door closed. Then he grabbed Abe's shoulders, slammed him against the wall, and took his mouth in a scorching kiss. He licked, bit, and sucked on Abe's lips before pushing him to his knees.

"I know what you're doing," Jason said breathlessly as he untied his waistband and dropped his pants.

"What's that?" Abe leaned forward and mouthed Jason's erection through his briefs.

"You're distracting me so I give in and let Kristen go on a date." He frantically shoved his underwear down with one hand and gripped Abe's hair with the other. "It isn't going to work."

"The distraction is a fringe benefit." Abe lapped at Jason's balls. "We'll talk about Kris when we're done."

His patience for conversation exhausted, Jason gripped his cock and painted Abe's lips with it. "Open," he said hoarsely.

Without protest, Abe parted his slick lips and took Jason in. He wasted no time before sucking on Jason's glans and flicking his tongue over the surrounding skin.

"I won't last long," Jason warned.

With a groan, Abe clutched Jason's thighs, increased the suction, and took his cock in deeper. "Mmm, mmm," Abe moaned in ecstasy as he worked Jason past the point of no return.

"Oh Christ. Abe." Jason pinned Abe to his groin as his lungs seized, his muscles tensed, and his balls emptied. "C'mere," he said once his cock stopped pulsing cream into Abe's waiting mouth. "C'mere." He helped Abe to his feet, flicked open the button on his shorts, and then shoved his hand inside and took hold of his cock. "Cum for me, baby," he said before covering Abe's mouth with his own and thrusting his tongue inside.

Abe grabbed Jason's shoulders and screamed into his mouth as he shot, coating Jason's hand with his release.

"That's it, baby." Jason stroked Abe's cock. "That's it."

His body limp, his eyes closed, and his chest heaving, Abe leaned against the wall.

"God." He sucked in air. "Wow." He opened his eyes and met Jason's gaze. "Thanks."

Smiling, Jason leaned forward and kissed Abe's cheek. "You're very polite and incredibly gorgeous." He licked Abe's lips. "That was hot as hell." He sucked on Abe's neck. "But I'm not letting Kristen date."

"Ever?" Abe said with a laugh as he stepped out of his flip-flops and shoved his shorts and briefs down. "Don't you think that's a little extreme?"

"No, not ever, smartass." Jason pinched Abe's butt before divesting himself of his own clothing. "But she's too young."

"You're telling me you didn't date at her age?"

"That's different," Jason said as he scooped up their clothes and walked into the closet.

"How's it different?"

"It just is." He put the clothes in the hamper and then went into the bathroom.

"Because she's a girl?" Abe took his shorts out of the hamper and put them on, leaving off the underwear.

If Kristen and Donny weren't downstairs, he'd try to get them both up for round two. Shaking his head to clear away the thought,

Jason said. "Not because she's a girl." He walked into the shower stall. "Because she'll be dating boys." He turned on the water and stepped under the spray.

Abe threw his head back and laughed.

"Laugh at me all you want," Jason said. "I know what teenage boys think about all day, and I'm not letting them near Kristen."

"And what do they think about?" Abe asked.

"Sex," Jason answered simply. He poured shampoo into his palm and rubbed it through his hair. "And maybe sports. But mostly sex." He rinsed his hair, reached for the soap, and lathered his body.

"That's a bit of an exaggeration."

Jason coughed, "Bullshit."

"But even if it's true, do you think forbidding Kris from dating is going to change the boys or how they think?"

"Change? No." Jason washed the soap off his body and turned off the water. "But if they can't get to her, she'll stay safe."

Abe held Jason's towel open as he stepped out of the shower. "You know this isn't a good plan, right?" Abe asked softly, gazing up at him. "You realize she'll find another time or place to see whoever this guy is and that in all likelihood her mother isn't going to be this strict?"

Grunting, Jason took the towel and rubbed it over his body. "So your suggestion is that at fifteen she should be allowed to go gallivanting around the streets at all hours of the night completely unsupervised?"

"Uh, wow." Abe blinked rapidly and cleared his throat. "I'm glad we're up here instead of having this conversation in front of anyone, because that comment would have lost you credibility."

"I don't need credibility!" Jason tossed his towel over the rack. "I'm her father."

Abe pressed his lips together tightly, but then his cheeks puffed and he broke into laughter.

Realizing he sounded ridiculous, Jason sighed. "Fine."

Wiping tears from his eyes, Abe kept laughing.

"All right. All right." Jason wrapped his arm around Abe's waist and tugged him close. "You can cut it out now." He nuzzled Abe's neck. "Why don't you tell me what you think I should do?

That's where this is all going anyway, right?" He kissed Abe lightly. "Let's hear it."

"I think—" Abe cleared his throat, chuckled, and then continued speaking. "I think you should ask Kris who the guy is and what their plans are. If he's a kid from school and they're going somewhere public, she's doing what every other kid her age does. Plus, you can drive her to wherever she's going and pick her up a couple of hours later."

The plan sounded reasonable. Jason grunted.

"Get dressed." Abe smiled at him. "I'll go downstairs and make sure dinner's under control."

"Fine." Jason walked to the closet and looked at Abe over his shoulder. "And I noticed you didn't put any underwear on."

"I wasn't hiding it." Abe winked and swung his ass from side to side. "I need to find some way to hold your attention in a room full of loud people."

"That'll never be a problem," Jason assured him.

Abe's expression turned serious. "Never?"

Jason met his gaze. "Never."

Chapter **14**

ABE WAS used to change. He had moved from family-values Salt Lake City to anything-goes Las Vegas at age eighteen. When some of his friends from home had been on church missions or getting married, he had been with new friends at parties and in clubs where drunkenness and random hookups were common. He had been raised with the assumption that one day he'd marry a woman and have a family, and then he had changed his parents' plans for his future by announcing that there would be no Mrs. Green.

Considered in that context, the progression of his relationship with Jason and his children wasn't the biggest lifestyle change Abe had experienced. But there was still a period of adjustment, for him and for Jason.

Thankfully, working with teenagers all day had given Abe perspective about how they functioned and patience when dealing with them. Both of those skills came in handy when Angela called him frantically one Thursday in mid-July.

"Hi, Angela. What's going on?" he asked, wondering why she was calling him in the middle of her workday. Although he had gotten to know her better over the past couple of months—chatting when the kids were being dropped off and meeting for dinner a couple of times to compare notes on Kris and Donny—she didn't usually call him, and when she did, it wasn't from work.

Angela's work ethic was as strong as Jason's. She also shared Jason's sharp intelligence and sometimes sarcastic sense of humor. The more time Abe spent with Angela, the more he understood why Jason respected and adored her. Abe felt the same way.

"I hate to ask you to do this, but Jason is in surgery all morning and I have a scheduled C-section I don't want to hand off to one of my partners. The patient's been with me for two other births and we have a good rapport."

"Tell me what you need and I'll take care of it," he said. "I'm not busy."

Summer break was Abe's time to keep current on new teaching trends, put together lesson plans to match his curriculum, and attend meetings with the school staff and administration. Most of those things he did from home, and his deadlines were self-imposed. That summer he had added moving to his task list, but he was done with that and waiting for Jason to notice.

"I got a call from the club. Donny's been in a fight. They're being really understanding about it, or they're at least pretending to be understanding about it because of the exorbitant membership fee I pay, but they said he needs to be picked up right now and he can't come back until Monday."

Though he wished that information was surprising, it wasn't. Donny didn't say much to him or anybody else, but Abe watched him as subtly as he could. The boy was sullen, angry, and clearly heading for trouble. Dealing with students was different than dealing with his boyfriend's child. His own stepfather had been a big part of his life, but Abe hadn't yet figured out where the lines were with Jason's kids. It seemed he had to stop looking for lines and start talking openly with Jason before Donny made a mess his parents couldn't get him out of.

"What happened?" Abe asked.

"I don't know, exactly. They didn't give me details. They just said to come get him and keep him out of camp tomorrow too. It's fine for him to stay home alone tomorrow, but leaving to go pick him up now is impossible unless I cancel my afternoon."

"No problem. I'll go get him," Abe said, walking to the closet to get his flip-flops. "I'll leave now. Does he know to expect me?"

"I'll call over there to let him know. Thanks again, Abe. I realize this isn't your responsibility."

"He's Jason's son," Abe said as he shoved his wallet in his back pocket. "That makes him my responsibility."

Angela made a sound that sounded like a gasp and then said, "That's—" She cleared her throat. "That's really wonderful. Thank you."

"Anytime," he said sincerely. "I'll send you a text when I have him to let you know everything's fine. Do you want me to pick Kris up today too? They're coming over tomorrow anyway, so we can just make it a night early. That way I'll be around and Donny won't have to be home alone." Not that Donny would complain about being home alone. In fact, Abe guessed he'd prefer it, but that didn't mean it was the best thing for him.

"You don't think Jason will mind? I'm sure you two have plans tonight."

Having the kids over meant no blow jobs in the kitchen or fucking over the back of the couch, but otherwise, their plans for the night would stay the same. On the surface, Abe wouldn't have thought he'd have a lot in common with an arrogant surgeon who picked him up at a bar, refused to exchange more than cursory information, and made it clear he had no interest in pursuing a date, let alone a relationship. But now that he knew Jason well, Abe realized they were very well-matched when it came to most things, including how they liked to spend their time.

They were both homebodies, preferring quiet evenings at home to loud bars or restaurants, especially during the workweek. After the first time they'd watched a movie on Jason's big-screen TV instead of at the movie theater, Jason had bought a popcorn maker and a case of Milk Duds and implemented naked movie night. Which was another area where their needs met in a way Abe had never dared to hope would happen. His sexual fantasies had always been just that—fantasies. The idea that a man could be rough and dirty with him in bed but still respectful and gentle out of it had seemed too contradictory to be realistic. And because Abe absolutely needed the latter, he assumed the man he'd end up with wouldn't be able to give him the former. Being with Jason showed him both were possible.

"We don't have any plans," Abe said. "Jase probably won't get home until close to seven, and then we're having lasagna and watching whatever Netflix recommends."

"That sounds… really domestic and sweet, actually. If you're both okay with Donny and Kris coming over a night early, that would be helpful," she said and sighed. "I need to go. But, Abe?"

"Yes?" He walked into the garage and hit the button to open the door.

"I'm really glad Jason met you. You've been great to my kids and—" She cleared her throat. "I'll always love Jason. Our marriage was destined for failure, but he's my friend and I've worried about him for so long. I never thought…. You're good for him. He's a happier man, a better man, with you in his life."

Warmed soul-deep at those words but unsure how to respond, Abe went with simple but honest. "He does the same for me. I'll, uh, text you soon."

"Good. Thanks again. Bye, Abe."

"Bye."

"IT WASN'T my fault!" Donny screamed from the family room.

"I didn't say it was your fault!" Jason yelled back.

"It's what you meant!"

"Don't tell me what I mean! I know what I mean!"

"How were your classes today?" Abe asked Kristen as he sat next to her in front of the peninsula in the kitchen.

"Good." Kristen looked over her shoulder to the commotion in the other room and then bit her lip.

"Is your lasagna okay?" Abe asked, trying to refocus her attention.

"What?" She glanced down at her untouched meal. "Oh. Yes. Sorry." She scooped a bite up with her fork, placed it in her mouth, carefully chewed it, and then swallowed. "This is very good. Thank you, Abe."

Her words were exceptionally polite, but her smile was forced and her eyes were tense.

"He's going to be okay," Abe said quietly.

"I think he's—" She snapped her mouth shut, reached for her glass, and gulped down her water.

"You think he's what?" Abe asked.

"Fine! What did you mean?" Donny shouted from the family room.

"I asked you what happened today," Jason said. "That's what I meant!"

"And I told you it wasn't my fault."

"Dammit, Donny. Answer my question. I want to know why you got into a fight."

"Because the guy was an asshole and he started it, that's why."

"Watch your language," Jason scolded.

"Are you kidding? You just said 'damn' and I can't say 'asshole'?"

After a momentary pause during which Abe flinched, Jason said, "I'm an adult."

"Oh, so you didn't say 'asshole' when you were my age?" Donny snorted disbelievingly. "Yeah, right."

"Don't use that tone with me, Donny."

"Or what? You'll send me back to Mom's house? She doesn't want me either."

Abe winced and closed his eyes. The boy needed to be in therapy. Yes, it was possible the problems were mostly due to hormones he'd eventually outgrow, but eventually was too far away and he could do irreparable damage in the meantime.

"You're not going to distract me with a pity party, Donny. I want to know what happened today."

"And I already told you, I don't know. It wasn't my fault." There was a thumping sound, and Abe hoped whatever Donny had thrown, kicked, or hit didn't do any damage. "You know what?" Donny yelled. "Forget it. I don't need this. I'm going to my room!"

"Donny!" Jason called after him.

Hard, rapid footsteps sounded on the stairs and Donny didn't respond.

"Donny!" Jason shouted again. After a pause, the front door opened and slammed shut.

Abe took in a deep breath, let it out, and said, "Kris, what were you saying earlier?"

Flicking her gaze away, she said, "I, uh, think Donny's getting worse."

She was probably right. "Your parents know he's having trouble, and they're going to help him."

She didn't look as if she believed him, and Abe wasn't sure anything he said would change that. The reality was, things had to change with Donny before any of them would feel better.

With no easy solution available, he tried distraction and bribery. "I have cookies for dessert. They're my grandmother's award-winning recipe. But we have to finish our dinner first." He looked meaningfully at Kristen's plate. "There seems to be a break in the noise, so let's eat."

"What about Dad and Donny?" she asked.

"Donny's upstairs and your dad went for a, uh, walk. They can warm up a plate in the microwave when they calm down."

"Okay." They ate in silence for a few minutes, and then Kristen said, "Abe?"

"Yes?"

"I'm glad you're here. I didn't like being alone when Donny yelled like that."

It was the second time that day a member of Jason's family had expressed happiness at his presence, which made him feel like there was space for him in their lives. "I'm glad I'm here too." He reached over and patted Kristen's hand. "It's going to be okay."

She nodded and refocused on her dinner. Abe did the same. When they were both done, he stacked their plates and stood up. "I'll get the cookies."

"That's okay," she said. "I'm not really hungry and I have homework to do, so I'm going to my room."

Understanding Kristen's need to be alone, Abe nodded. "Good night, Kris."

"Good night." She shuffled out of the kitchen with her head down.

Abe sighed. They had to do something to improve the situation.

"THIS GOES down in history as being the crappiest night ever," Jason grumbled as he walked into the bedroom.

After cleaning up the kitchen, Abe had gone upstairs, gotten ready for bed, and climbed under the covers. He read a book while he waited for Jason to come home.

"The mouth on that boy." Jason growled and kicked his shoes off so hard they hit the wall. "Sorry." He took in a deep breath. "I didn't mean to do that."

"It's okay," Abe said as he sat up, the blanket pooling at his waist. He put a scrap piece of paper in his book and set it on the nightstand. "You're allowed to be upset."

"Angela's worried," Jason said with a sigh. "Really worried."

"You called her?" Abe asked, holding his hand out.

"Yeah." Jason looked at him. "That's what took me so long out there. That and the pacing." He sat on the bed next to Abe and brushed his hand through Abe's hair, his touch gentle. "Sorry I took off like that."

"That's okay." Abe cupped Jason's cheek and skated his thumb over his lips. "Going outside to cool down was probably the best thing you could have done."

With a sigh, Jason lay back, his head on Abe's lap, his knees bent, and his feet on the floor. He threw his forearm over his eyes and said, "I don't know what I'm doing with them. I feel like I'm fucking them up."

"You're not fucking them up," Abe assured him as he combed his fingers through Jason's hair and then began massaging his scalp. "At least not any more than most parents. You wouldn't be doing your job if you didn't give them something to complain about to their friends."

"Ha-ha," Jason said.

Though his tone was sarcastic, the tightness around his mouth was replaced by a small smile, so Abe hoped the comment helped. Abe continued pressing his fingers into Jason's scalp.

"That feels good, baby," Jason said.

After a few more minutes of quiet massaging, Abe said, "Jase?"

"Yeah?"

Setting aside his worry about Jason's reaction, he said, "Can I make a suggestion about Donny?"

Rather than tensing or arguing, as Abe expected, Jason said, "Please." He moved his arm and blinked his eyes open. "I meant what I said, Abe. I have no idea what to do about him."

"I think you need to go to counseling."

"He won't go. Remember? Angela tried."

"Not him. You, meaning the collective you. Family therapy."

Jason shot up to a sitting position. "I don't need therapy!"

Unable to hold back his amusement, Abe smiled.

"Are you laughing at me?" Jason asked defensively.

"I adore you," Abe said. He crawled out from under the blanket and climbed onto Jason's lap, straddling him. "I really do, you know." He gazed into Jason's eyes. "There's nothing wrong with therapy, and if you believe there is, I'm not sure how you can expect Donny to think something else."

"I didn't say there was anything wrong with therapy." Jason's posture relaxed, and he wrapped his arms around Abe, resting them on his bare ass. "But I don't need it. I'm fine."

Skipping the obvious correlation between that comment and Donny's own refusal to get help, Abe kissed the underside of Jason's chin and said, "Your family needs it. Maybe if you make it about the family instead of about Donny, he'll go."

"Do you think that'll work?" Jason knit his eyebrows together.

"I do." Abe nuzzled Jason's neck.

"Okay. I'll try that. Hopefully he'll go for it."

"If he doesn't, you can still see the therapist. I bet someone who specializes in adolescents would have good advice for you about how to help Donny at home and how to encourage him to come in for an appointment." He kissed the underside of Jason's chin, buried his hands under Jason's shirt. "I can ask the psychologist who works for our school district for recommendations."

"Yeah, okay," Jason said. "I'd rather not ask people at work."

Hiding his smile against Jason's neck, Abe lapped at his salty skin. The apple really didn't fall far from the tree with Donny. In this case, it meant both father and son were temperamental and stubborn when it came to asking for help, but hopefully it also meant Donny would grow into a good man like his father.

"I'll get you a couple of names." Abe rucked Jason's shirt up his chest. "But try to remember that if you think there's something wrong with needing therapy, Donny will too." He kissed the center of Jason's collarbone.

"Uh-huh," Jason murmured distractedly, raising his hands so Abe could push his shirt off.

When Jason's cock hardened underneath his ass, Abe decided it was time to stop talking. They'd covered all the high points anyway. He pushed Jason's shirt over his head, latched on to Jason's nipple, and sucked while he worked open the button and zipper on Jason's pants.

"That feels good, baby." Jason tightened his hold on Abe's backside, digging into the muscles and encouraging Abe to rock closer. "Mmm."

They moved together languidly, neither pushing to quicken the pace. Abe worked Jason's nipples over while Jason focused on Abe's ass—first the globes, with hard rubs, then the crease, with gentle strokes, and eventually the hole, which Jason circled with his fingertips.

"What are you in the mood for tonight?" Jason whispered.

"You." That was always the answer and always the truth. Anything he did with Jason, everything he did with Jason, turned Abe on and made him soar. "Want you," he mumbled into Jason's mouth before slipping his tongue inside.

The kiss burned hot from the start. Jason grabbed Abe's hair and tugged him forward, taking his mouth ferociously as he increased the pressure on Abe's hole and popped his fingertip inside. Abe went wild on top of him, biting his lips, scratching his back, and humping against his belly.

"Fuck. Abe. Baby." Jason nipped at Abe's chin and shoved him onto the mattress.

"What?" Abe asked, his mind a haze of arousal and confusion.

"Need to get these pants off," Jason said as he climbed off the bed.

Abe propped himself up on his elbows and watched Jason shove his pants and briefs to the ground. When Jason lifted one foot to reach for his sock, his dick bobbed enticingly, and Abe rolled onto his side, leaned over the bed, and swiped his tongue over the dark, slick glans.

"Christ." Jason grabbed the base of his dick with one hand and Abe's jaw with the other, forcing Abe's mouth open as he pushed himself past Abe's lips and deep into his mouth. The angle was different, which made Abe gag, but Jason didn't slow down. "Take it," he growled as he slid over Abe's tongue. "Fucking choke on it."

Abe's balls drew up, and for a moment, he thought he was going to cum, completely untouched, just from Jason's taste and scent and dominance. But he breathed in deeply through his nose, calming himself, and managed to take Jason in deeper.

Firmly but gently, Jason nudged Abe onto his back and raised his hands above his head. Keeping one foot on the floor for leverage, he tossed his other leg over Abe's shoulder, trapped Abe's arm underneath it, and braced his knee on the bed. He kept his hold on Abe's face with one hand and used the other to pin Abe's free arm down.

"Try to move," he ordered.

Abe tugged his arms halfheartedly, having no desire to get away.

"That's it," Jason said. "I have you." Still holding Abe's head in place, he began rocking in and out of Abe's mouth as he gazed down into Abe's eyes, his expression blissful but harsh. "You make me so hard, baby," he said as he thrust. "Turn me on so much."

Completely entranced by the man above him, all Abe could do was stare and moan as he sucked.

"Look at you." Jason ran his thumb over Abe's spit-wet chin. "Drooling for me."

Whimpering, Abe arched his back, desperately wanting friction on his dick.

"Here's what we're going to do," Jason rasped, dragging his erection back and forth over Abe's tongue while he spoke. "I'm going to fuck your mouth, cum in it, and then—" He breathed in deeply. "You're going to lie there and I'm going to ride your cock until I cum again."

Abe bucked and cried out, the sound muffled by the hard shaft in his mouth.

"Yeah," Jason said. He held Abe's head in place and moved faster, deeper. "Knew you'd get off on that." Early seed seeped onto Abe's tongue, making his cock throb and his balls ache. "Which one do you like better, dirty boy?" Jason asked breathlessly. "Swallowing me down or fucking me?"

A tear leaked from Abe's eye, the emotion and need he felt for this man too much to contain. His touch soft, Jason skated his hand up, wiped the tear with this finger, and then raised it to his mouth and sucked on it. Moved by the tender action, Abe relaxed his arms and neck, leaving himself completely at Jason's mercy.

"That's it," Jason whispered. He moved quickly after that, stretching Abe's lips, pushing at his throat, and turning him on. Then, just as he was about to cum, Jason reached back, grabbed Abe's package, and squeezed hard.

"Ungh!" Abe shouted around the pulsing dick in his mouth. "Ungh!"

Jason squeezed again, and Abe exploded, cum shooting out of his cock while he swallowed down Jason's load.

"Mmm." Jason moved off Abe's heaving chest and lay down alongside him. "You make me crazy," he said quietly as he leaned forward. He licked Abe's neck and gently fondled his balls. "Completely crazy."

"You can talk about that with the therapist," Abe joked, his voice weak as he worked to fill his lungs.

Jason's lips curled up. "No way am I telling anyone what my hot little teacher's like in bed." He flung his arm over Abe and drew him near. "Don't want anyone to take you from me."

"Not going to happen." Abe snuggled close.

"You bet your ass it won't." Jason brushed his mouth over Abe's. "And to make sure of it, nobody gets to know about this side of you except for me." He bit Abe's lower lip and husked, "You're mine."

Abe had never felt safe enough to share that part of himself with another man. Jason didn't use flowery words or make grandiose gestures. He had a stubborn streak, a hair-trigger temper, and trouble recognizing emotions. But he made Abe feel cherished, protected, and free.

"I'm yours," Abe agreed in a whisper.

Chapter 15

"DID YOU already shower or do you want to join me?" Jason asked as he rubbed circles on Abe's lower back.

"I already showered and I want to join you." Abe kissed Jason's chest, gave him a final squeeze, and sat up. "You made me all sweaty."

"I plan to get you sweaty again after the shower, baby." Jason dragged his fingers over Abe's cock and around his glans. "I'm going for a nice, deep ride, remember?"

His breath catching, Abe nodded. "Uh-huh."

Grinning with satisfaction, Jason swung his legs over the side of the bed and got up.

Jason didn't bottom often, but occasionally he seemed to be struck by the mood to be filled, and then he turned the tables. If ever there was a man who topped from the bottom, it was Jason. It made Abe hot, but then everything about Jason did that.

"Are you coming?" Jason asked, looking over his shoulder.

"Yeah." Abe shook his head to clear it and stood. "Yes." He followed Jason into the bathroom, scooping up clothes from the floor along the way and then tossing them into the hamper. By the time they got into the shower, his brain was mostly operational again. "How was your day?"

"Other than finding out my son got into a fight and then coming home to a yelling match?" Jason asked.

"Yeah. Other than that," Abe said with a smile.

"Not bad." Jason picked up the soap, lathered it, and began washing Abe's shoulders and chest. "There was one awkward moment when a patient's husband and a family friend got into an exceptionally polite fight."

Furrowing his brow, Abe asked, "How is a fight polite?" He got his hands soapy and slid them over Jason's torso.

"Well, everyone was nicely dressed and kept their voices low, but the husband wouldn't stop asking the friend why he was there, and the friend did everything he could to stand closer to the wife. Then things got even worse when the friend's wife came and smiled at everyone while shooting daggers with her eyes at her husband."

"What did you do?" Abe asked.

"I tried my usual trick of imagining them naked and bent over so I wouldn't have to focus on what they were saying." He snaked his hands around Abe's chest and washed his back. "That works in almost every situation, but the passive-aggressive comments got to be too much after a few minutes, so I went to the nurses' station and told one of the nurses to clear the room. She let the patient choose one person to stay, and the rest of them had to go to the waiting area."

"Uh." Abe's hands froze over Jason's hips. "I have a couple of questions."

"What?" Jason moved Abe's hands down to his dick.

Cupping his hands over Jason's package, Abe said, "Your usual trick when dealing with difficult patients is to imagine everyone's naked butt?"

"I don't limit that trick to patients. And I don't imagine everyone naked." Jason slid his hands down Abe's back and lathered up his ass. "I only do it with men."

"Fine. Your usual trick to deal with awkwardness is imagining guys bent over?"

"Bent over. On their knees. On their backs." Jason shrugged. "I'm not picky." He waggled his eyebrows. "But I am blessed with a great imagination." He squeezed Abe's ass.

"You're a major perv." Abe gently massaged soap over Jason's balls with one hand and stroked it onto his cock with the other.

"And you love it."

"Ehm. I, uh—" Abe dropped his chin and looked up at Jason from underneath his lashes. "Maybe."

"Definitely." Jason smirked. "What was your other question?"

"My other question?"

"You said you had two questions."

"Oh." Abe soaped up Jason's balls. "Right. Who did she choose?"

"Who did who choose?" Jason asked in confusion.

"The patient. You said the nurse was only going to let her to choose one person to stay in the room and she'd kick the rest out. Did she choose her husband or the friend you think was really her boyfriend?"

"That was the best part." Jason's smile was huge. "She picked the friend's wife."

"Seriously?"

"Swear." Jason made a symbol of a cross over his heart.

"That is awesome." Abe laughed. "I bet the husband and friend were livid."

"I have no idea," Jason said. "All I know is their imaginary naked asses don't hold a candle to yours." He pinched Abe's butt and then backed into the water.

"Awww," Abe said with chuckle. "Aren't you sweet?"

"Yes. Now let's finish up in here." He stepped out of the spray, groped his semihard dick, and shook it at Abe. "I'm ready for the next round."

"Wow." Abe moved under the water and got his hair wet. "And they say romance is dead."

"You want romance or you want my ass wrapped around your cock?"

Abe decided romance was overrated. He stopped making jokes and hurried to finish the shower.

BY THE time Abe finished washing up and drying off, Jason was already in the bedroom. Abe walked in to find him sitting on the bottom corner of the bed, his legs spread and his dick hard. The urge to drop to his hands and knees and crawl over to worship that perfect cock was huge.

"Uh-uh-uh." Jason shook his head. "You can have this later." He ran his palm languidly over his erection. "C'mere."

His heart pounding and his belly tightening, Abe walked over to Jason and stepped between his thighs.

"You really are gorgeous," Jason whispered as he took hold of Abe's hips and dragged his gaze over Abe's face, chest, and groin. "I love the way you're put together." He bent forward and blew hot breath on Abe's balls, up his cock, and over his glans. "Let's get you ready to go."

Abe was well past ready, but he didn't argue when Jason opened his mouth and dropped it over his cockhead. "Jase," Abe moaned. He put his hand on Jason's head, gently petting as he enjoyed the feeling of Jason's hot mouth and soft tongue sucking and licking his cock.

Jason rolled his balls and slowly bobbed up and down his shaft, keeping him aroused and needy. "All right, baby," Jason said once he pulled off Abe's cock. "Time to glove up." He reached for the condom and lube sitting next to him on the bed, covered Abe's dick, and then slicked him up with a few strong strokes. "Let's switch spots."

With his hands on Abe's waist, Jason stood up, turned them around, and set Abe on the corner of the bed. He straddled Abe's thighs, one of his legs on each edge of the bed, and looked down at him. "You better brace yourself." He put one hand on either side of Abe's neck and then moved them up to his head. "I want it hard."

Abe shuddered in response, too turned on to speak.

His lips curled up in a wicked smile, Jason climbed onto the bed, planting his knees next to Abe's butt. He lowered Abe down until he was lying on his back with Jason looming over him, and then he reached behind himself and held Abe's dick up. "Here we go," Jason rasped as he squatted down and pressed his hole against Abe's cockhead.

Knowing Jason liked to control the show, even from this end, Abe lay still and watched the intense concentration, grimace of pain, and relief of pleasure skate across Jason's face as he sat down and took Abe's cock deep inside his hot, tight body.

"Fuck, yes," Jason groaned. He closed his eyes and arched his neck. "That's so good."

"Jase!" Abe cried out as he bucked and grabbed on to Jason's thighs.

"Oh no you don't." Jason opened his eyes and smirked at Abe. "This is my show." He grabbed Abe's wrists, raised his hands next to his head, and held them in place. "You have a nice cock, baby." Jason gazed into Abe's eyes as he moved up and down. "Fills me just right." He circled his hips, putting pressure on Abe's balls and adding new friction to his cock.

Whimpering, Abe tried to stay still and keep breathing. "Jase," he said hoarsely.

"Yeah?" Jason raised his ass until just Abe's glans was inside and then dropped back down hard.

"Ah!" Abe shouted and squirmed.

"That's it," Jason said as he rose again. "Dance for me." He dropped down, ground himself against Abe, and shifted back up. "Give me a good ride."

With his hands pinned to the mattress and his legs hanging over the side of the bed, Abe had a limited ability to move, but he thrust up underneath Jason as much as he could, stabbing himself into tight heat as he moaned and whimpered. They both breathed harshly, their chests heaving and nostrils flaring. Abe watched Jason's erection slap against his belly and the muscles in his legs and stomach flex as he undulated above him.

"I'm close," Abe said when his balls tightened. "Going to cum."

Jason squeezed his ass around Abe's cock and quickened his pace, pulling Abe into a strong climax.

"Jase!" he shouted triumphantly as seed sprayed from his cock. "Yes. Yes. Yes."

When Abe finally finished shooting and collapsed onto the mattress, Jason released his hand, took hold of his own dick, and stroked himself to completion. "Yeah," he grunted as white cream flowed over his fingers. "Ungh, yeah." After a few seconds, Jason took his hand off his dick and wiped it on the sheet. He leaned over Abe and grinned. "Thanks for the ride."

Abe snorted breathlessly. "Anytime."

Jason climbed off Abe and removed the condom. "Get into bed." He nudged his chin toward the top of the bed. "I'll get something to clean you up."

"'Kay," Abe said, his chest heaving. "Soon as I can move. My legs don't work yet."

"That's because I am *good*." Jason waggled his eyebrows and then sauntered into the bathroom.

Too satisfied to come up with a snappy response, Abe just sighed contentedly. He closed his eyes and listened to the water in the bathroom as he waited for Jason to come back.

"I really wore you out, didn't I?" Jason said as he wiped Abe's groin with a soft cloth.

Abe opened his eyes and met Jason's adoring gaze.

"Let's get under the blankets." Jason kissed him and tossed the washcloth aside.

Together, they scooted up the bed and lay down, Jason's arm around Abe's shoulders and Abe's head on Jason's chest. Happy, sated, and warm, Abe fell asleep.

JASON'S SCHEDULE on Fridays had shifted to earlier start times so he could be home by a little after five. He left Abe in bed with a soft kiss, a friendly grope, and a "Have a good day, baby."

Though Abe tried to fall back asleep, without Jason's thick, warm body tangled with his, all he could manage was a few restless minutes of shut-eye. With a resigned sigh, he threw his blanket off and went into the bathroom to start his day.

When he shuffled into the kitchen at eight, Kris was already there, books and papers spread in front of her.

"Good morning."

"Hi, Abe." She smiled at him.

"What are you doing up?" he asked. "Your class doesn't start until ten on Fridays, right?"

"Yeah, but I went to bed early and I couldn't sleep anymore, so I figured I'd study."

THE HALF OF US

He grinned and shook his head in amusement. "You are a dream student."

She ducked her head, but her eyes twinkled and she was smiling, so Abe knew she appreciated the compliment.

"Your last class ends at two today?" Abe asked as he got a mug out of the cabinet.

"Yes. But I can stay in the library and study until someone can come pick me up. That's what I usually do."

"I'm doing pickup today, and I'll be able to get you at two." He picked up the carafe and poured the warm brew into his mug, leaving plenty of room for milk.

"It won't disrupt your day?" she asked.

"No." Abe shook his head as he stepped over to the refrigerator and grabbed the milk. "I have a little bit of work to do, and then I'm going shopping for your dad's birthday present."

Jason's birthday was in exactly one week, on July 31, and Abe had to figure out what to buy for the man who could afford anything.

"What are you getting for him?"

"I don't know yet." Abe took a sip of his coffee and winced. He'd prefer a chai latte, but he couldn't make that at home, and Jason always had the coffeemaker set the night before, so the coffee was easier. "Your dad's not an easy man to shop for."

"I have an idea," Kris said excitedly.

"What?" Anything that made her that happy would be a strong contender.

"You can get him one of those fancy coffeemakers."

"What's wrong with this coffeemaker?" Abe asked, pointing to the shiny machine on the counter.

"Both you and my dad make a face when you drink that coffee, so I'm guessing it's not very good. But that's not what I meant, anyway. My friend Ilia's parents have a machine that uses those little plastic cup things and makes all sorts of flavors. We use it to make hot chocolate when I spend the night at her house. It even has that milk-frother thing."

"Hmm," Abe said as he pressed his lips together and nodded. "That's not a bad idea."

"It's a great idea," Kris said, displaying some of her father's charming self-confidence. "My dad will love it and the rest of us can use it too."

"I always said you were exceptionally smart." Abe walked over to the sink and poured his coffee down the drain, no longer in the mood to suffer through a mediocre beverage now that he was thinking of fresh-brewed, flavored drinks. "That's what I'll get him from the three of us."

"The three of us?"

He nodded. "You came up with the idea, so your name has to go on it and I, uh, bet your brother would have said so too if he was here."

She rolled her eyes at that last comment. "Yeah, right."

"I'm going upstairs to do a little work and then I'll drive you to school. We can stop at the Roasted Bean on the way," he said cheerfully. "It'll be a farewell trip, because once we get our fancy new coffeemaker, we'll become our own baristas."

THOUGH IT was tempting to avoid Donny, Abe stopped by his room on his way downstairs. "Donny," he said as he knocked on the door. "I'm taking Kris to class and then going to the mall to get your dad's birthday present. Do you want to join me? We're stopping by the coffee shop on the way."

Abe was expecting to be ignored or to hear a loud no from behind the door, so he stumbled back in surprise when, instead, Donny yanked the door open.

His hair was sticking up in all directions, and his tattered, baggy jeans barely hung on his hips. "I need to stop by Mom's house to get my things," he said as he pulled a wrinkled T-shirt over his head. "You can take me, right?"

"Oh. Sure. Of course."

"'Kay. I'll be right down." He rubbed his hands over his bleary eyes, scratched his head, and flicked the door shut as he turned around.

Frustrated at the rudeness but wanting to choose his battles with the strong-willed boy he was still getting to know, Abe sighed and went downstairs.

"Ready?" Kris said when she saw him.

Her brown hair was neatly brushed and pulled into a tight ponytail. She was wearing a tan skirt that hit her knees, a pink polo shirt, white shoes, and her backpack. Everything about Jason's children, from their demeanors to their wardrobe, was different. It kept life interesting.

"Yes, but we're waiting for Donny."

"Donny's coming with us?" she asked in surprise.

"Yes. He needs to pick up some things from your mom's house."

She frowned.

"Do you need something too?" Abe said, thinking that was what upset her. "I know I picked you up a day early unexpectedly."

"No." Kris shook her head. "We've been keeping clothes and toothbrushes and everything here all summer. What would I need to pick up at my mom's?"

Based on Kris's tone, Abe realized her frustration was related to her brother. He hoped that once Donny got help, his mood would stabilize and their relationship would improve.

"Let's go," Donny said as he trudged down the stairs. From the look of his hair, Abe assumed he hadn't bothered to run his fingers through it, let alone brush it.

Kristen followed, her shoulders tense, and Abe made a mental note to get referrals to therapists that day.

THE MORNING passed by relatively smoothly. They stopped at the coffee shop and got drinks and pastries, dropped Kris off at the community college, and then went to Angela's house, where Donny ran inside. Abe waited in the car and used the time to send some texts asking for referrals to therapists and then forwarded the responses to Jason. After fifteen minutes, Donny came back with a bag, and Abe drove toward the mall.

"Where are we going?" Donny asked.

"Shopping, remember? We're getting your dad a birthday present."

Frowning, Donny said, "Can't you drop me at home?"

"It'll be fun," Abe said. When that response resulted in a scowl, Abe tried another approach. "I'm not great with electronics, and I want to get him an espresso machine." He flicked his gaze toward Donny. "I know you're good with your games and computers, so I was hoping you could help me pick one out."

"Oh." Donny didn't smile, but he seemed less upset. "Sure. Whatever." Donny reached for the radio and turned on the music.

Relieved that they were making progress, however small, Abe didn't bother Donny for the rest of the drive. By the time they got to the mall, Donny seemed less tense. He grunted more than he spoke, but he helped pick out the espresso machine for his father and chose some of the capsules they'd use for drinks. It was almost one by the time they had the wrapped gift in their hands, and Abe was able to talk Donny into getting lunch at the food court while they waited for Kris's class to finish.

"What do you want to eat?" Abe asked.

"Pizza. That's my favorite food."

Pleased that Donny had volunteered information about himself, Abe tried to continue the conversation. "Oh, yeah? It's your dad's favorite too."

"It is?" Donny looked interested at first, but then he schooled his expression. "I mean, whatever."

Ignoring the last comment, Abe said, "Yes. Do you like it cold or just hot?"

Donny shrugged and buried his hands in his pockets as they continued walking.

"Because your dad likes both. Have you ever noticed how he always orders too much when we get pizza delivered?"

"Yeah." Donny glanced at him.

"That's so he can eat cold pizza the next day."

"Oh." Donny looked away, but not before Abe saw a small smile on his face. "I like to do that too."

"You guys have a lot in common."

"It's just pizza."

"That and you look like him."

"People say I have my mom's eyes."

Abe twisted his head to the side. "I can see that. But you've got your dad's build and his hair too. Same color and thickness, plus"—Abe pointed at his own forehead—"both of your hairlines are pretty straight across the front, but then they dip up at the ends."

"I, uh, never noticed that."

"I spend a lot of time looking at your dad," Abe said before he realized the comment might make Donny uncomfortable.

"He spends a lot of time looking at you too."

Surprised but pleased at the response, Abe smiled. They reached the pizza place, walked through the order line, and then carried their trays to a nearby table.

"So you're, like, living with my dad now, right?" Donny asked between bites of pizza.

Treading carefully, Abe said, "Would that be okay with you?"

"Sure. Whatever." Donny shrugged. "Lots of kids have stepparents."

Given all the internalized shame and anger Jason'd had when they'd first met, Abe knew Angela was responsible for the easy acceptance her kids exhibited. With as much as Jason thought he did wrong, marrying such an amazing woman and having two great kids hadn't been a mistake.

"Want to hear something funny?" Abe said.

Donny looked up from his plate, his expression interested. "Yeah."

"I'm living with your dad, but he doesn't realize it."

"What do you mean?" Donny asked from around a mouthful of fries. He had ordered a large basket of them in addition to two slices of pizza. "You're always there."

Abe laughed. "Yes. I'm always there. My clothes are in his closet and my toothbrush is next to his sink, but it all happened slowly, and he doesn't notice a lot of things or think about them."

"Uh, doesn't he notice you never go home?"

"Not yet." Abe reached over to Donny's tray and snagged a fry. "I used to sublet a room from a friend, but a couple of months ago, she got engaged and gave notice on her lease. I thought about finding someplace else but, like you said, I'm always at your dad's. Most of my clothes were there by then, anyway, so I boxed up my books and the rest of my things and rented one of those small storage units for them."

Donny laughed. "That's funny."

"He'll figure it out eventually. Your dad's smart." Abe picked up his tea and took a sip. "Just like you."

"Like Kris, not like me."

"Your sister's brilliant," Abe agreed. "But so are you."

Donny smiled again and pushed his basket of fries toward Abe.

ABE RETURNED home that afternoon with two seemingly happy teenagers and a great birthday gift. All in all, it had been a nice day.

And then all hell broke loose.

He was in the kitchen, figuring out what to make for dinner and waiting for Jason to get home, when he heard loud noises from upstairs, followed by both kids shouting. Immediately, he ran out of the room and up the stairs.

"Let go of it, you bitch!" Donny shouted.

"No! You can't do this," Kris said.

Their voices were coming from the bathroom, along with the sound of a scuffle. Abe hurried in to see Kris on the floor, huddled over the toilet and reaching for the handle, and Donny curled over her, grasping at her hand.

"You guys! Stop!" he yelled as he ran into the room.

Donny lunged forward and scratched Kris's arm, causing blood to bubble to the surface.

Kris cried out in pain.

"Donny, let go." Abe came up behind him and tried to get a grip on his arms or back. "You're hurting her. Let go."

"Get off me!" Donny yelled.

"Abe!" Kris shouted, sounding terrified.

"Donny, stop. You don't want to do this." Abe's heart raced with fear, but he managed to grab both of Donny's shoulders and yank him back, giving Kris a little more room. "Get out from there, Kris," he said breathlessly, the effort of holding Donny back and the adrenaline pumping through him causing his lungs to ache.

"I can't!" She wriggled and tried to move, but she was still pinned between the toilet and her brother.

Abe braced one foot against the wall behind him and pulled harder. "Donny, let her go!" He managed to yank Donny back farther, but instead of running away, Kris darted up, grabbed the handle, and flushed the toilet.

"No!" Donny yelled and lunged toward Kris, but Abe held on as hard as he could.

"Kris, get out of here!" he shouted again, and finally she listened, crawling away a few feet and then getting up and running out of the room.

Donny went wild, wiggling and shaking. "You can't get away from me!" he yelled at his sister. "Get the hell off me!" he shouted at Abe. "You had no right!"

Abe wasn't sure who the last comment was directed toward, but it didn't matter. The effort of holding Donny down was wearing on him, and he knew the boy would get loose sooner rather than later. "Donny, calm down and tell me what happened."

"He's a stupid druggie!" Kris shouted from the doorway. "I found drugs in his bag!"

Abe's world stopped spinning with that revelation. He knew Donny had problems, but he had no idea it had gotten to that level. And like a fool, he had taken Donny to get that bag, no questions asked. He felt sick but tried to keep himself together. "Kris, go downstairs and call your father," he said, each word an effort.

"Fuck you!" Donny shouted. "You had no right to go through my things."

"Kris, go!" Abe yelled hoarsely.

"Get off me!" Donny said, managing to get one shoulder free.

"I will if you calm down," Abe said. "We'll figure this out. Please calm down."

"Fuck you, faggot! Get off me." Donny shifted from side to side and then threw his elbow back, landing a direct blow in the center of Abe's chest and knocking all the air from his lungs.

The punch sent Abe flying backward into the wall. He grabbed his chest, trying and failing to catch his breath. Curling into a ball, he thought back to the tricks he'd learned to deal with a severe asthma attack, something he hadn't suffered since childhood. He focused on slowing his breathing, inhaling through his nose, and exhaling out of his mouth, but he couldn't get enough air in his lungs, and his vision started going hazy.

"Kris!" Donny yelled, his voice sounding far away. "Kris, come here! Something's wrong with Abe."

By the time footsteps sounded and Kris's soft hand landed on his forehead, he knew even his inhaler wouldn't help because he wouldn't be able to suck hard enough to get the medicine into his lungs. He looked up at her and tried to focus, but everything was getting gray.

"Donny! Call 9-1-1," she said. "I don't think he can breathe."

Chapter 16

ONE OF the most terrifying moments of Jason's life was pulling up
to his townhouse and seeing an ambulance out front. He parked next
to the curb and hurried out of his car just as the ambulance drove
away.

"Dad!" Kristen yelled and ran over to him. She fell into his
arms and sobbed. "Abe's hurt. He can't breathe."

Jason made a living staying calm in traumatic situations, but
he suddenly found it impossible to focus. "What happened?" he
said. "Never mind. Did they say where they're taking him?"

"Saint Rose," Kristen said. "I want to come with you."

"Okay, let's go." He opened his car door and started getting
back inside.

"I'll be right back. I need to get my shoes." She turned around
and darted into the house.

"Dad."

Jason glanced up and saw Donny shifting from foot to foot, his
hands in his pockets and his gaze averted. "Can I come too?" he
asked.

"Yes." He looked at Donny's feet. "Get your shoes and lock
the front door on your way out."

Once all three of them were in the car, he drove to the hospital,
his hands trembling. Wanting to make sure they got there in one

piece, he skipped conversation and focused on keeping to a reasonable speed and avoiding an accident.

The short drive seemed to take forever, and then he struggled to find a parking place. By the time Jason walked into the emergency department, his nerves were shot. "I'm with Abraham Green," he said to the front-desk nurse. "He was brought in by ambulance."

"Are you family?" she asked as she turned toward her computer and began typing.

Making a mental promise to get medical powers of attorney in place right away, Jason said, "Yes."

"Take a seat and I'll have someone walk you back."

Though his first instinct was to yell, ask for the chief of staff, or start making phone calls to someone who could tell these people who he was, Jason managed to keep himself in check. "Kristen, Donny, go over there." He pointed them toward the vinyl couches in the corner. "I don't know how long I'll be, so call your mother and tell her what's going on."

"We can't go back there with you?" Kristen asked, her eyes bloodshot and swimming with tears.

"No." He shook his head. "One person at a time." Which wasn't necessarily true and really depended on Abe's condition and what they were doing to treat him, but Jason didn't think it would help his kids or Abe to see each other in that setting.

"You're with Mr. Green?" a woman said from behind him.

"Yes." Jason swung around.

"Follow me."

"Kristen, call your mother," he said and then followed the woman down the hall and hoped for the best.

It didn't take long before they reached a heavy door. They walked through, passing two curtained-off emergency rooms, and then the nursing aide pulled the curtain on a third room and stepped aside to let Jason in. Abe was reclining on the bed with an IV in his arm and an oxygen mask with a nebulizer attachment over his nose and mouth. He was pale but didn't have any obvious signs of injury. Apparently the sound of footsteps got his attention, because he opened his eyes.

When their gazes met, Jason flashed back to that first night in the bar almost a year earlier. The one-night stand he'd picked up had somehow turned into the center of his world. Suddenly, his chest ached and his stomach heated, which should have made him turn around to find the nearest doctor and demand a scan and a physical, but it felt too good to be sickness.

Jason had loved people in his life. His children, Angela, his parents, his sisters, his nieces and nephews, his grandparents, and probably others. But he had never been *in* love. Not until that moment. Or at least he hadn't realized it until that moment. He'd probably been feeling it for months.

His heart pounding with joy, hope, and, yes, a little panic, he pushed the revelation aside to be dealt with later. Right then, he needed to check on Abe. "Hi, baby," he said softly as he stepped toward the bed. "You gave me quite a scare."

Lifting the mask off his face, Abe asked, "How're the kids?"

"Put that back." Jason hurried his pace and replaced the mask over Abe's nose and mouth. "The kids are fine and breathing is important." Jason darted his gaze around until it landed on a chair. He reached his leg out, hooked his foot over the metal bar at the bottom, and pulled it over. "Nonverbal answers only," he directed as he sat down and leaned on the bed. "Are you feeling better?"

Abe nodded and put his hand on top of Jason's.

"Good." Jason sighed in relief. He grinned and shrugged sheepishly. "I guess that's the only yes or no question I had."

Abe smiled at him from underneath the oxygen mask and squeezed his hand just as his phone rang.

"Crap," Jason said. "I forgot to put it on vibrate." With his free hand, he fished the phone out of his pocket and ended the call before registering that Angela's name was flashing on the screen. "That was Angela." He stood up. "I'll be right back, okay? I need to call her and make sure she's on her way here to get the kids."

After nodding, Abe squeezed his hand one more time and let go.

Jason hit the Send button as he walked out of the room and searched for a hallway away from the patient-care area.

"Is everything okay?" Angela asked, answering the phone on the first ring. "What happened?"

"My guess is an asthma attack, but I don't know what triggered it." He dragged his hand through his hair. "It isn't usually this bad. I haven't seen the ER doctor yet or gotten the story from Abe." He drew in a deep breath. "The good news is he's fine."

"Good," she said, sounding relieved. "I'm on my way to pick up the kids. Do you need anything?"

"No." Jason shook his head reflexively. "I'll text you when I know more."

FOUR HOURS later, Abe was signing discharge paperwork, and Jason texted Angela to let her know they were heading home and Abe was fine. The albuterol, oxygen, and rest had returned Abe's lung function to normal, but Jason still didn't know what, if anything, had triggered the attack because they hadn't had a moment alone together. He blamed the overly friendly emergency doctor for that problem. Honestly, with the amount of time the man had spent looming over Abe, it was a wonder he had been able to treat any other patients.

"Ready to go?" Abe asked from behind him.

"Yes." Jason dropped the phone in his pocket. "Isn't your new friend going to come give you a hug good-bye?"

Immediately, Abe started laughing and then coughing. "Quit it," he said. "I'm too tired to laugh and you're too cocky to be jealous."

"I'm not jealous," Jason said. They walked toward the exit doors. "I'm just pointing out that the doctor had a not entirely professional interest in you."

"He's married," Abe said. "I saw the ring."

"So was I," Jason countered. "And why were you looking to see if he had a wedding ring?"

"I wasn't looking! It was just there." He shook his head. "You're cute but silly. The guy was doing his job. That's all."

"I'm not cute and his job doesn't include staring at patients." They left the hospital and headed toward the car.

"He's supposed to treat me without looking at me?" Abe asked as he threaded his arm though Jason's and leaned against him.

"He wasn't looking. He was staring."

"Ah. I see." Abe paused. "How does one discern the difference?"

"You were there. Don't tell me you didn't notice how he kept looking into your eyes every two seconds."

"Okay. Eye contact during conversation equals lust." Abe nodded. "Got it."

They reached the car and Jason opened Abe's door. "The guy was coming on to you," Jason said. "I'm an expert on the subject, so you'll have to take my word for it."

"I'm familiar with your come-on technique, and as I recall it was something like, 'You want to go home and fuck?'" Abe said as he got into the car.

"I was more suave than that. Otherwise I wouldn't have landed you." Jason winked and carefully shut the door. He jogged to the driver's side, climbed in, and turned on the ignition. "Okay. We're alone, with no interruptions." He backed out of the parking space and started the short drive home. "Tell me what happened. Is the pollen count high? Did your allergies set you off?" When Abe didn't respond, Jason flicked his gaze to the side. "Abe? What happened?"

"I'd never keep something involving your kids from you, but I'm fine, so—"

"My kids?" Kris couldn't find her way to trouble with a GPS device on a one-way road. Jason clenched his jaw. "What did Donny do?"

"Jase, I'm—"

"What did he do?"

With a sigh, Abe said, "It was an accident and I'm sure he's sorry."

They drove in silence for a few minutes while Jason gathered his thoughts. "I used to worry what Kristen and Donny would think of me because I'm gay," he said, his voice low but steady. "Angela told me over and over that it didn't matter, that I was their dad and who I dated had nothing to do with how they felt about me." He tightened his grip on the steering wheel and ground his teeth. "But it impacted how *I* felt about me, so I didn't believe her. When she filed for divorce, I assumed I'd never be able to live the life I'd planned. I thought I'd be alone with no family."

Abe didn't interrupt, but he reached across the console and put his hand on Jason's thigh.

"But now that's changed." Jason put his hand on Abe's. "You changed that." He cleared away the sudden thickness in his throat. "I don't want you to decide being with me is too hard."

"I won't," Abe assured him. "I love being with you and your kids. They're not going to drive me away."

"Good." Jason sighed in relief and rolled his shoulders, trying to shake off the tension that had been bogging him down. "But Donny isn't a baby anymore. He's thirteen and he needs to learn to behave." He swallowed hard. "I'm his father. It's my job to make sure that happens."

"You're right," Abe said. "We're almost home. Can we talk about this after I take a shower and get the hospital smell off me?"

"Yes." Jason grinned at him. "I'll even wash your back."

THE BUZZING phone woke Jason the following morning. By the time he figured out what the noise was, it had stopped. But then it started again a couple of seconds later. He didn't want to wake Abe, who was lying on his chest, so he gently shifted to the side until Abe was resting comfortably on the mattress. Then he got up, snagged the phone, and checked the display as he walked out of the room. Before he could return the three missed calls he had from Angela, the phone started vibrating in his hand.

"Hello," he said quietly.

"Hi, Jason. We're in front of your house. The kids have their keys, but I didn't want you to worry about who was coming in, so I wanted to call you first."

"What time is it?" he asked.

"Seven." She sighed. "I'm sure you had a late night, but they did too. They're very concerned about Abe."

"All right." He rubbed his palm over his temple and tried to wake up the rest of the way. "Come on in but keep them downstairs. I'll wake Abe and we'll be down there in a few minutes."

"I'm awake," Abe said hoarsely when Jason stepped back into the bedroom. He sat up and blinked rapidly. "What's going on? Is everything okay?"

Even sleep-rumpled and tired, Abe took Jason's breath away. With no way to avoid the obvious, Jason admitted to himself that he had fallen hard. But this time he felt no panic, only a desire to shelter, protect, and touch.

"Everything is fine." Jason sat on the bed and trailed his fingers across Abe's jaw. "Kristen and Donny were worried about you, so Angela brought them over. If you're too tired to—"

"I'll take a nap later." Abe pushed the blanket down. "They must feel terrible. I need to show them I'm okay and tell them I'm not upset."

Touched beyond measure by how much Abe cared for his children, Jason wrapped his arms around him and pulled him into a hug. "You amaze me," he whispered. He kissed Abe's neck. "I'm furious with both of them. Kristen should have come to us instead of taking matters into her own hands, and Donny...." He shook his head and sighed. "I don't even know where to start with Donny. But here you are, barely out of the hospital and thinking about them." He nuzzled Abe's warm skin and knew he wanted to do that for the rest of his life. All those childhood dreams and desires he had abandoned long ago surged to the surface of his consciousness with a vengeance. "We need to talk, baby."

"You know how much I like *talking* with you." Abe snaked his hand between them and rubbed it over Jason's erection. "But your kids are downstairs waiting for us, so I'll need a rain check."

"I really did mean talk." Jason chuckled. "The hard-on's just inevitable when you're naked." He nipped Abe's ear. "Or clothed." He released his hold and said, "Okay. Let's go."

A FEW minutes later, they were both dressed and walking down the stairs.

"Abe!" Kristen shouted as soon as Abe entered the family room. She ran over, fell into his arms, and burst into tears. "Are you okay? I'm so sorry."

Jason knew how much Kristen adored Abe, so her reaction
didn't surprise him. What did take him off guard was Donny
hustling over to Abe almost as quickly as his sister and, when Abe
opened his arms, joining the group hug.

"I'm sorry," Donny said, his voice rough. "I didn't mean it."
He blinked rapidly and cleared his throat. "I don't know why I said
it, but I swear, I didn't mean it, and I wasn't trying to hurt you. I...."

"It's okay," Abe assured him. "I know."

Donny tucked his face against Abe's shoulder and trembled. "I
thought you were dead. I thought I killed you."

"I'm fine." Abe looked up and met Jason's gaze. "It was an
accident. You got me help and stayed with me. I know you didn't
mean it."

"Okay, everyone." Angela walked in from the kitchen holding
a bag from the bagel store and a stack of plates. "Time to get off
Abe and eat breakfast." She glanced at Jason. "I figured if we were
going to invade your house at an ungodly hour on a Saturday, the
least we could do was bring bagels." She set the bag and plates on
the coffee table in front of the couches. There's cream cheese in the
bag, and the bagels are presliced." She walked back toward the
kitchen. "What does everyone want to drink?"

"I'll have coffee," Jason said. "Abe?"

"Water's good."

"Kristen, will you please help your mother with drinks?" Jason
said.

Kristen sniffled, nodded, and followed Angela.

Donny stepped back from Abe too, but he turned away and
dipped his chin, averting his face.

Unsure how to approach his son but aware that he had to do it,
Jason stepped close to him and said, "Donny?"

"Yeah?"

"Abe told me what happened."

Donny's shoulders slumped and he curled in on himself.

"I made an appointment with a therapist," Jason continued. He
had actually made the appointment before the previous day's

excitement, but that detail wasn't important. "I realize you haven't been willing to—"

"I'll go," Donny said. He slowly turned around and lifted his gaze. The usual anger and indifference were gone, replaced by sorrow and regret. "I didn't mean to hurt Abe." He swallowed thickly. "I didn't."

"I know," Jason said. His boy suddenly looked younger, more vulnerable. "But you did hurt him. And your sister. You could have hurt that kid from your camp. And you could have been arrested for the pot." Jason moved toward Donny and cupped the back of his neck. "Abe suggested that maybe a family therapist would be a good idea. I talked with your mother about it, and we agree." They'd also agreed to start searching Donny's room and his things. But that was a fact to share in front of the trained professional. "We've had a lot of changes lately. You and Kristen are spending more time here. Abe is in our life now." Jason flicked his gaze to Abe and said, "And hopefully he'll be moving in, so—"

Donny snorted and grinned. "*Hopefully*."

Abe smiled broadly.

Confused by their reaction, Jason looked at Abe and arched his eyebrows in question.

"Cindy got engaged in April," Abe said. "Her lease on the apartment ran through the end of May. I remembered what you said once about her wasting rent when she spent all her time at her boyfriend's house, so instead of finding a new place, I moved in here." His eyes twinkled. "I hope that's okay."

"Oh." Jason thought that comment over. He wanted Abe with him every day and every night. "Good."

Donny snorted again.

Apparently having overheard the conversation, Angela walked up holding two coffee mugs. She handed one to Jason and said, "When's the appointment with the therapist?"

"Thursday at five," Jason said. "She said she wants to meet with the entire family together the first time. Does that work for you or should I change it?"

"It works." Angela nodded. "I'll put it on my calendar."

"Abe?" Jason asked.

"Yes?" Abe looked at him.

"Thursday at five. Family therapy. Can you make it?"

Abe's smile was radiant. "Yes." He looked at Kristen, Donny, Angela, and finally Jason. "I'll be there."

Epilogue

"MERRY PRETEND Christmas," Jason whispered into Abe's ear. He pressed his chest to Abe's back, pushed his leg between Abe's thighs, and curled his arm around Abe's waist. "Have you been a good boy this year?"

They had taken the kids to Reno for Thanksgiving with Jason's parents, which meant Angela had them for Christmas. Abe and Jason were flying to Salt Lake City the next day to spend the actual week of Christmas with Abe's parents, sister, and the rest of his family, so they'd decided to do an early celebration in Henderson with Kristen and Donny. But it was early, so the kids were still asleep and they had time for fun of their own.

"That depends." Abe mumbled sleepily as he wiggled his ass against Jason. "Is Santa going to give me a better gift for being on the naughty list or the nice one?"

"You're getting a reward either way." Jason cupped Abe's balls and rolled them gently while he began sliding his cock against Abe's ass. "But first, Santa needs to slip his present into your chimney."

Laughing, Abe twisted his head over his shoulder and looked at Jason. "I want your, uh, present in my chimney, but next time we role-play, I get to choose the characters."

Jason bit Abe's shoulder and smiled. "No problem." He licked his way up the side of Abe's neck and nibbled on his earlobe while he caressed his chest, stomach, and groin. "As long as you're the one in bed with me, the rest is just window dressing."

Abe rolled onto his back, gazed up at Jason, and cupped his cheek. "It still makes my heart race when you say things like that."

"Good." Jason turned his face and kissed the inside of Abe's wrist. "I'll make sure to keep it that way." He climbed over Abe and settled between his spread legs, bracing himself on his forearms.

With his blue eyes focused on Jason, Abe circled his arms around Jason's neck and tugged him down for a kiss. Their lips met with gentle brushes and soft licks, and when Jason slanted his mouth over Abe's and pushed his tongue inside, Abe moaned and wrapped his legs around Jason's waist. The change in position allowed Jason to slide his cock into Abe's warm cleft. Groaning with pleasure, he began to slowly rock his hips.

He was so focused on Abe's taste and heat and scent that he didn't notice Abe reaching for the lube until he handed it to him. "Need you," Abe rasped, his pupils wide and his lips red and swollen. He scooted his feet higher on Jason's back, tipping his pelvis up and improving Jason's access to his hole.

"I need you too," Jason said. He flipped the cap on the lube, poured some into his palm, and then closed it and tossed it aside as he reached between his legs and slicked up his throbbing shaft. With no further delay, he pressed his cockhead to Abe's pucker and pushed forward until he broke through and began to glide into smooth, tight heat.

As Jason breached him, Abe's mouth dropped open and his nostrils flared, but he never looked away from Jason's eyes. "Yes," he said, arching his back when Jason was fully settled inside. "Fuck me."

With their relationship firmly established, they had stopped using condoms, which Jason adored. But he enjoyed the other impact on their sex life even more—he could still be wild and dirty with Abe; he could hold him down and ravage him; he could pull his hair and pinch his nipples; he could fuck his mouth and his hole with his tongue, fingers, and cock. But he could also hold him close, kiss him tenderly, and make love to him gently. Whatever they did together in bed brought them closer, connected them further, and allowed Jason to worship Abe in every way he could imagine.

And that morning, it was a slow, easy fuck. They rocked together, running their hands over each other's body, licking over each other's lips, their hips connecting and releasing with every thrust. When Jason knew he was close, he reached between their bodies and took hold of Abe's cock.

"Going to fill you up, baby," he said as he pulled on Abe's dick and pumped into his ass.

"Jase!" Abe cried out. He dug his fingers into Jason's shoulders and tightened the hold of his legs around Jason's waist. "Don't stop," he said frantically as he pushed up against Jason's dick, taking him in deeper and harder. "Please don't stop."

Though he wanted to stay inside forever, Jason's balls were drawn up and his belly was tight, telling him the inevitable was coming.

He stroked Abe faster, pounded into him harder, until, with a final gasp, Abe threw his head back and yelled, "Ah! Jase! Yes!"

Abe's seed shot across Jason's belly at the same time he came deep inside Abe's body.

"That was the best present ever," Abe said breathlessly. He grinned mischievously. "Thanks, Santa."

Jason rolled to his side and took Abe with him, holding him close. "Ho ho ho."

A COUPLE of hours later, the gifts were opened, the family room was trashed, Kristen was on the phone with her friend, and Abe was in the kitchen fighting with the fancy espresso machine he'd gotten Jason for his birthday five months earlier.

"Aren't you going to help him?" Donny asked. He was sitting next to Jason on the sofa watching TV.

"How do you suggest I do that?"

"Show him how to use the machine," Donny responded, his tone and expression making clear he thought the answer was obvious.

"If I knew how to operate that stupid machine, I wouldn't have been late to work two days this week."

"You don't know how to use it either?" Donny said disbelievingly. "How is that possible? You're a doctor."

Jason slowly turned his head toward Donny. "Let's call a spade a spade here. That machine is ridiculous, and nobody except the manufacturer's representative knows how to use it." He refocused on the TV. "Personally, I don't think she knows, either. I'm convinced they edited the video on their website to make it look like she made the perfect latte when in reality, she just picked it up at Starbucks like the rest of the country."

"Dad, it's an espresso machine from Williams-Sonoma, not a space missile. You put in the cup, press the On button, and then, if you want, you can use the milk steamer. That's it."

"Jase!" Abe shouted from the kitchen. "It's making that hissing sound again!"

"Throw it in the trash!" Jason yelled without moving from the couch.

"No. I already told you, we're not throwing it away. Come help me."

"Christ," Jason grumbled as he got up. "Coming."

He walked into the kitchen to see Abe standing arm's distance from the machine and holding a cup under the frother. "Do you hear that sound?" Abe asked. "What's happening?"

"How should I know?" Jason threw his hands over his head. "Maybe it's finally doing us a favor and exploding."

Abe looked at him, his eyes wide. "Do you really think it's exploding?" The machine sputtered loudly, and Abe jumped away. "Oh my God! I think it's exploding."

"You guys are embarrassing." Donny marched into the room, took the mug from Abe's hand, and stepped over to the machine.

"Donny, don't!" Abe warned. "We think it's exploding."

With a shake of his head and a disgusted sigh, he fiddled with a knob, tapped his foot, and then turned around and thrust the mug at Abe. "Here. All done."

"Oh." Abe took the cup and glanced down at it. "That looks… good." He smiled at Donny. "Thank you."

The boy grunted and stomped back to the couch, muttering under his breath. "Pathetic."

"Who're you calling pathetic?" Jason called out after him. "I had to come up with an alias for the iTunes account because I was too embarrassed to order that ridiculous music you wanted for Christmas."

"What's going on in here?" Kristen leaned over the peninsula, her phone still at her ear. "Nothing. I was talking to my dad," she said to her friend. "I told you the same thing! It's like my mom always says, once a cheater, always a cheater." She turned around and walked toward the family room. "Okay. I'll pick you up in an hour."

"This is good," Abe said as he sipped the drink. "Here, try it."

He handed the mug to Jason, who took it reflexively. His mind was stuck on Kristen's comment. "Abe?" he said quietly.

"Yeah?" Abe came over and put his hand on Jason's hip. "What's wrong?"

"I won't cheat on you." He put the mug on the counter, wrapped his hands on either side of Abe's neck, and gently petted him with his fingertips. "I know they say once a cheater, always a cheater, but that isn't true, or at least it isn't for me." He licked his lips and gazed into Abe's eyes. "I'm not going to make excuses for what I did before, but I swear to you, I'm not that guy anymore. Not with you."

"I know," Abe said softly. "I do know."

"Yeah?"

Abe nodded and leaned close to him, "Aside from the fact I'm all over you so often I'm not sure you could get it up to cheat on me—"

"Hey!" Jason pulled back, affronted. "I have no problem—"

"If you ever even think about cheating," Abe said, grinning disturbingly, "I'll cut off your dick while you're sleeping and throw it out the car window on the side of the freeway."

Jason gaped.

"Uh, you were a little scary right there," Kristen said. "I mean, not to me, but if I was my dad, I'd be scared."

Jason flipped around and saw Kristen standing next to the peninsula again. "You shouldn't eavesdrop," he snapped.

"Are you kidding me? I was taking notes so I can give Abe's advice to Ilia." She paused and tilted her head to the side thoughtfully. "Can you really cut off a dick?"

"Kristen!" Jason shouted.

"Sorry." She rolled her eyes. "I meant to say 'penis.' Can you really cut off a penis?"

Exasperated, Jason shook his head and said, "Google it. That freeway idea wasn't Abe's. It's been done."

"Seriously?"

Jason nodded.

"Be right back." Kristen hurried out of the room.

Turning back to Abe, Jason said, "So, what were we talking about?"

"Uh, Jase?"

"Yeah?"

"Did you just tell your sixteen-year-old daughter to go Google 'cut penises'?"

His stomach dropped and he ran after Kristen. "Kristen! Wait! Don't pull up any pictures. I need to see your results before you click on anything. Kristen!"

Behind him Abe laughed and said, "Gotta love having a family."

CARDENO C.—CC to friends—is a hopeless romantic who wants to add a lot of happiness and a few "awwws" into a reader's day. Writing is a nice break from real life as a corporate type and volunteer work with gay rights organizations. Cardeno's stories range from sweet to intense, contemporary to paranormal, long to short, but they always include strong relationships and walks into the happily-ever-after sunset.

Cardeno's Home, Family, and Mates series have received awards from Rainbow Awards, the Goodreads M/M Romance Group, and various reviewers. But even more special to CC are heartfelt reactions from readers, like, "You bring joy and love and make it part of the every day."

You can learn more about Cardeno's writing at http://www.cardenoc.com/.

The FAMILY Series

SOMETHING
IN THE
WAY HE
NEEDS
CARDENO C.

A BOOK IN THE *Family* SERIES

http://www.dreamspinnerpress.com

STRONG
ENOUGH

CARDENO C.

A BOOK IN THE *Family* SERIES

http://www.dreamspinnerpress.com

The FAMILY Series

http://www.dreamspinnerpress.com

The HOME Series

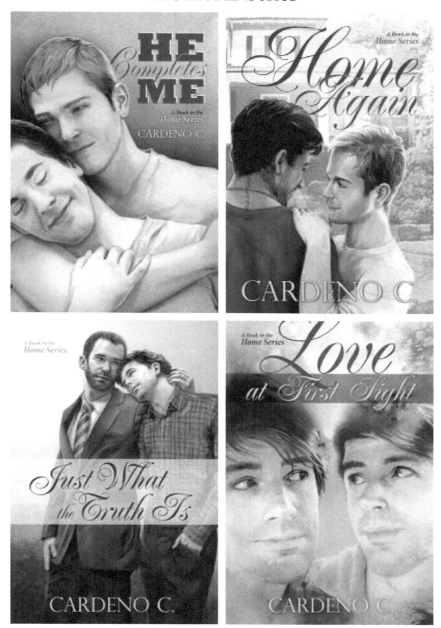

The HOME Series

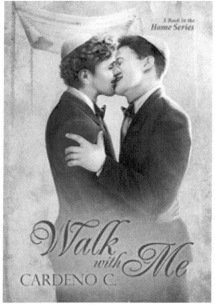

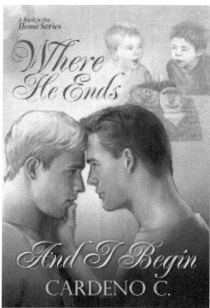

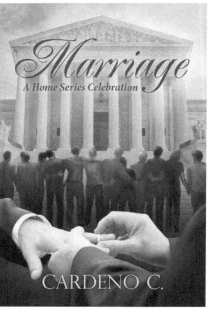

http://www.dreamspinnerpress.com

The MATES Series

A BOOK IN THE MATES SERIES

*W*ake
ME UP INSIDE

Two men, destined
for each other

CARDENO C.

http://www.dreamspinnerpress.com

The MATES Series

A BOOK IN THE MATES SERIES

Until
FOREVER COMES

CARDENO C.

http://www.dreamspinnerpress.com

A BOOK IN THE MATES SERIES

IN YOUR

Eyes

CARDENO C.

http://www.dreamspinnerpress.com

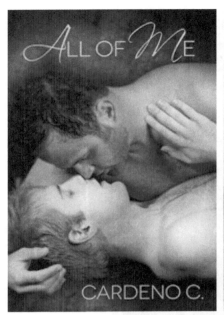

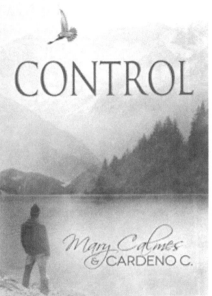

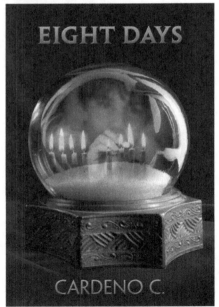

http://www.dreamspinnerpress.com

http://www.dreamspinnerpress.com

Perfect
IMPERFECTIONS
CARDENO C.

http://www.dreamspinnerpress.com

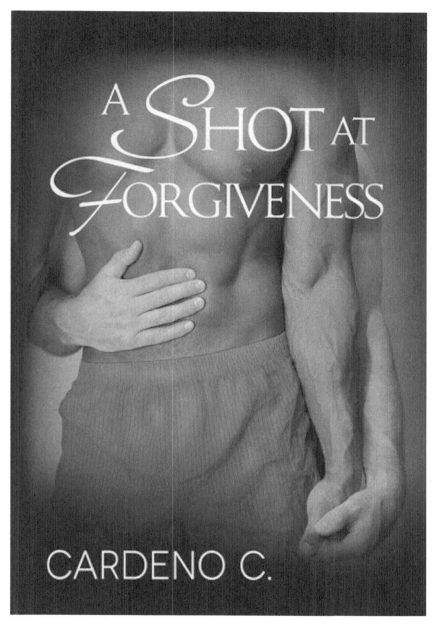

A Shot at Forgiveness

CARDENO C.

http://www.dreamspinnerpress.com

CPSIA information can be obtained at www.ICGtesting.com
Printed in the USA
LVOW01s0215291214

420708LV00019B/203/P

9 781632 163851